A PUZZLE OF POPPIES

A Sherwood & Jarvis Novella

Case No. 1

RENEE EDWARDS

This novella is a reimagining of Sir Arthur Conan Doyle's *A Study in
Scarlet*.

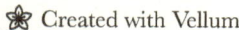 Created with Vellum

For Mollie, the best writing buddy I could have asked for.
I love and miss you, my sweet, ornery, precious kitty girl.

"They say that genius is an infinite capacity for taking pains," he remarked with a smile. "It's a very bad definition, but it does apply to detective work."

Sir Arthur Conan Doyle, *A Study in Scarlet*

Part I

FROM THE DESK OF
WILFRED A. JARVIS, M.D.,
ARMY MEDICAL DEPARTMENT,
66TH REGIMENT OF FOOT

Chapter 1

23 June 1880
  Bombay, India

MY DEAREST ESTHER,

Greetings from the far side of the world!

Even as I write this letter, I can imagine you opening it —a cup of tea at your elbow, Ella napping in her crib— and frowning down at the page because it has been so long since you wished me *bon voyage* with the strict instruction to write as soon as possible. Believe me, darling sister, when I say that I have done my best to comply with your dictum— it is only that all has been a whirlwind since we parted.

I hardly know how to describe Bombay to you. It is everything we imagined, poring over the atlas as children, and more. As soon as I disembarked from my steamer, legs still wobbly from my time at sea, I found myself caught up in the cheerful mayhem of the port, with street vendors and carriage drivers hawking their wares as crowds milled around before towering stacks of baled cotton. The more fashionable types from the ship made their way to the Byculla or Bombay Clubs, but those establishments seemed a bit rarified for the likes of me; instead, I found simple but agreeable accommodations in the environs of Malabar Hill. Not that I spend much time in them—the temptations of the city are too strong. The wide central roads, which are lined with a distinctive mix of stately, European-style buildings and more colorful structures constructed in the native fashion, give way to labyrinthine warrens of homes, market stalls, and temples. The heat is like nothing I have ever experienced, but palm trees sway in a breeze that is redolent of horses, wood smoke, and incense. Every sight, every sensation, is a thrilling reminder of how very far I am from home.

The real treasure of Bombay, though, is its people. Hindus, of course, predominate, but they are far from the only inhabitants represented. Bombay, I am told, is unique among Indian cities in its profusion of Parsis, so called because their forebears emigrated to the subcontinent from Persia. They follow the spiritual teachings of the prophet Zoroaster and are great philanthropists, responsible for much of the civic life in the city, which is also populated by Moslems, Jews, Sikhs, Jains, and more. Each group wears its traditional costume as a matter of course, and so the streets are alive with riotous silks and cottons, veils and turbans, painted faces and ornaments of gold. I cannot help but think that Father, who always approached foreign cultures and faiths with such curiosity and appreciation, would love it.

This morning, I woke early enough to visit the markets before their offerings had been picked over and purchased the most marvelous collection of pomelos, nectarines, and pistachios. I brought them back to the hotel with me, and they sit here on the desk as I write. When I finish, I shall make them my lunch while I watch the birds reeling around the Towers of Silence, which I can see from my open window. These towers, which are surrounded by lush, beautiful gardens, play a key role in Parsi funeral rituals. Rather than burying their dead, the Parsis carry the remains of their loved ones to the top of the structures, which are left open to the air. Following the appropriate rites and prayers, the cadavers are left behind, where their flesh is consumed by vultures. I have heard murmurings among the British in the city that this practice is barbaric, but I find it strangely beautiful. It seems far more in the natural way of things than constructing grandiose monuments of stone to mark a passing.

But I am becoming morose, and I cannot spare the time! I need to make the most of my residency here, for I am to leave posthaste. Upon my arrival in the city, I discovered that my regiment had departed for Afghanistan without me, and together with other officers in the same predicament, I will be setting out within the week to join the forces in Kandahar. My understanding is that we are hoping to cement our alliance with the new emir and drive Russian influence out of the region once and for all. I am nervous but also hopeful in anticipation of what this next chapter will bring. I will write you again as soon as I am able.

Your loving brother,
Wilf

Chapter 2

1 August 1880
Kandahar, Afghanistan

DEAR ESTHER,

I am afraid the tone of this letter is going to be a marked departure from that of my last missive. I am in Afghanistan, as planned, but every other expectation I had of my service here in the East has been dashed in a spectacular and calamitous manner. My military career thus far has proved, in the words of the philosopher, nasty, brutish, and short.

The journey from Bombay was uneventful, but just as we were getting settled in, word came down that we were to be dispatched to the Helmand River at the behest of the Wali of Kandahar to fend off an insurgency. We set out on the march to the rendezvous point with the Wali's forces, but as soon as we got there, things went horribly wrong. First, the Wali's troops mutinied, many of them joining the very insurgents all of us had been sent to fight. After that, there was confusion about our next steps until the order came down to proceed to the village of Maiwand, where we would ostensibly intercept the guerilla forces. Instead, the ensuing battle was a bloodbath, with the enemy outnumbering us five to one.

I will revisit the events of that day in my nightmares for the rest of my life. I saw too many men—good men, men I considered my friends—die horribly for no good reason. Our forces were ill-prepared for battle—the smooth-bore guns ran out of ammunition early in the afternoon, leaving us vulnerable—and once the insurgents were able to penetrate our lines, everything descended into chaos. I did what I could to aid the wounded, but at length, I joined their ranks when I was struck in the shoulder by a jezail bullet, which shattered my clavicle and grazed the subclavian artery. Murray, my orderly, threw me across a packhorse, and brought me safely to the British lines, but from there we still faced a long, arduous retreat to Kandahar.

I had thought Bombay hot, but it is a temperate oasis compared to the rocky desolation of Helmand. As such, the trip would already have been onerous, but with our water reserves entirely depleted, many of the battle weary were left on the brink of collapse. Word went 'round that a handful of desperate soldiers had broken into the rum casks in the baggage train and become so drunk that they could not keep up the march. They were allegedly left to their own devices of the plain, defenseless against the heat and the pursuing enemy. I cannot say what became of them.

During that long, painful episode, I thought often of Father's urgings to follow him into the ministry rather than take up the study of medicine. A part of me wished I could acknowledge to him that there may have been something to his reasoning, while another, more perverse portion was thankful that I never need do so—at least not until we are reunited in the hereafter. Eventually, our convoy did make it back to Kandahar; presently, arrangements are being made to send many of the wounded to the base hospital at Peshawar. I will write to you once I have arrived there and have a better idea of what lies in store for us.

Take care, darling sister, and give Ella a kiss from her uncle.

Your brother,
Wilf

Chapter 3

12 November 1880
   Peshawar, India

DEAR ESTHER,

   I can only hope that the relief you feel upon receipt of this letter equals the distress you must have felt for the months you have not heard from me. Once I explain my situation, sister, I think you will understand and, hopefully, forgive me.

   After I last wrote, we did indeed make our way to the hospital in Peshawar. My injury, though significant, responded well to treatment; I soon grew hale enough to walk about the wards, and even managed some time on the verandah, where I spent many a morning watching the sun rise and listening to the Moslem call to prayer. But then I was struck with enteric fever.

   The disease lingered for months, as is its wont. I am told that I was delirious for extended periods and experienced an intestinal hemorrhage at one point, but I remember very little of it, which is likely a blessing. I have only recently begun to improve. Even now, I am so weak that it taxes me to hold this pen, but I wanted to apprise you of my condition and future plans. The medical board has cleared me to return to England, and I will soon take my leave of India on the troopship Orontes, bound for Portsmouth.

I can see now how very naïve I was at the outset of this journey. It will be such a boon to find myself on English soil once again, and back in the bosom of family and friends.

Give my love to Ella and Basil. God willing, I shall see you all soon.

Your brother,
Wilf

Chapter 4

9 January 1881
London, England

DEAR ESTHER,

I know I told you before I left, but it bears repeating, just so I am sure you take my full meaning: it was so very, very lovely to spend Christmas with you, Basil, and Ella. I felt battered on the voyage home from India, in body and in spirit, but seeing you waiting for me on the dock in Portsmouth was a balm. I will be forever grateful for the warmth and care I received in your home as I began to recover from my ordeal. My time spent with Ella, in particular, was restorative. Watching her take in the world with her wide, innocent eyes and delight in each new discovery helped stitch together the jagged pieces of my heart. I have missed all of you terribly since arriving in the city and do not expect that to change anytime soon.

I am doing well enough here, I suppose. I have

consulted with friends from Netley about the therapeutic steps I should take for my shoulder and met up with some old colleagues of Father's who happen to be in town. Do you remember Rev. Anderson and his wife? They are departing for Canada, to plant one of the first Unitarian congregations in the province of Saskatchewan. I wished them well and assured them that Father would be most proud of them for delivering the faith to those who might find peace and guidance in it.

I also checked in at the War Office, for all the good it did. Nobody there has the slightest idea what to do with me—they seem hesitant to discharge me, but until I am fully recovered, I have no practical use in the field. This indecision has left me with far too much time on my hands, and I find myself slipping into bouts of rumination and lethargy. As it happened, I was in one such humour when I encountered an old school friend, David Stamford, and agreed to have a drink with him at a nearby pub; it is perhaps the reason I did not dismiss the proposition he made me out of hand. You see, Stamford is attached to the Foreign Office, and he told me he knew of a posting that I might find agreeable. It seems there is an embassy in need of a doctor, and because I am still an army man, in name, if not in actual practice, I could be dispatched to the office of the ambassador's military attaché without any disruption to my commission. The position would be on the island of Ynis Witrin, in service to the delegation assigned to Queen Mab of the Seelie Court.

I know what you must be thinking. This is hardly the kind of situation I ever aspired to; after all, the fae no longer have the same cachet they did in the years following Waterloo. But they are still our allies and… well, perhaps it is overly romantic of me, but I suppose I am drawn to the whispered possibility of adventure that we encountered as children, immersing ourselves in the stories of Arthur and Merlin, Beowulf and Robin Hood. It has been decades since the fae returned to the world, yet the Seelie Court remains an enigma. I've met army men who worked alongside the fae in the field, for extended periods even, who have a hard time relaying any information about the elfin peoples to others. These soldiers present the same distracted air and describe the same sensations whenever they are pressed to recount their experiences; their knowledge slips just beyond their reach, like an elusive name on the tip of their tongue. It's almost as if someone had orchestrated the phenomenon—say, by magic.

Some might take this hint of the uncanny as an excuse for malicious speculation and gossip, but I find it piques my curiosity, at a time when very little seems to pique anything in me at all. My trip to the East began with such promise, but my experiences there have ultimately left me feeling unmoored, lacking not only occupation but purpose. Even now that I am home, things that once brought me pleasure seem dull and grey (excepting your splendid company, of course). Perhaps in Ynis Witrin, I can find some small bit of wonder to give my world substance and color again. At the very least, I can try to do some good there—to build bridges instead of helping to make war.

Stamford told me the position is mine for the taking if I want it. I emphasized to him that I am not yet in a position to make any firm commitments, but that I am open to learning more about the role. I have received a preliminary message from one of the staff officers, a Captain Pryce, and I intend to initiate a correspondence to determine if this is an opportunity I truly wish to pursue. I will keep you updated on developments as they happen. Please, if you can, support me in this. I know it is not a path you would have chosen for me, but it seems to be the only one open to me now. Keep me in your prayers, and give Ella a kiss for me. I love you both.

Your brother,
Wilf

Part II

FROM THE DIARY OF
WILFRED A. JARVIS, M.D.,
ARMY MEDICAL DEPARTMENT,
OFFICE OF THE MILITARY ATTACHE
TO THE AMBASSADOR,
YNIS WITRIN

Chapter 5

6 March 1881

DEAR ESTHER,

I know this is not a letter. And I know you know it, too.

This is, in fact, the diary you gave me yesterday before you boarded the coach at the conclusion of our visit in Glastonbury. And when I told you that I had no use for a diary, that I would feel silly writing stories to myself, you looked so forlorn that I couldn't bear it, and I promised you I would try. So here I am, trying, because whatever my faults, I do not have it in me to break a promise to you, provided I have the power to fulfill it. And perhaps I will feel less ridiculous if I address these musings to you rather than myself or the ether.

It may be for the best, really. I have been told discreetly that while writing letters home from Ynis Witrin is not exactly forbidden, it is frowned upon—perhaps out of the same circumspect impulse that makes interactions with the fae so slippery to the human mind. Therefore, this could be my best and only chance to share my experiences with you.

I woke this morning with a peculiar feeling in my belly —something like the excitement of Christmas morning crossed with the fear and dread of an important examination. I rose and dressed quickly, gathering the few belongings that were not already packed in my trunks before descending to the inn's common room for a surprisingly excellent breakfast. As I was finishing my meal, I was hailed by the innkeeper and introduced to a local lad by the name of Nathaniel. The young man belongs to a nearby farming family and earns a bit of coin on the side by making deliveries to Ynis Witrin. On this day, he would deliver me.

As we set out, a misty rain cast a grey pall over the streets of Glastonbury, which did not strike me as a particularly auspicious beginning. Also, the site of my injury ached from the damp, as it so often does now, but it was tolerable, and I did my best to push my worries aside. Nathaniel was a man of few words, leaving me to watch the buildings slide by beside our wagon as we made our way through town and then further out to open country and toward Glastonbury Tor.

We were still a good distance out when the tor came into view, the great bulk of it looming over the surrounding plains. Even in the rain, I could see the abandoned tower of St. Michael's Church silhouetted against the clouds. Suddenly, I was overcome by an almost painful sense of immediacy and gravity. I was going to Ynis Witrin. That ancient place cherished by the peoples of Albion, Elfame, Annwn, and beyond; domain of Arthur in the Golden Age, when he forged the alliance between those peoples that lasted for centuries; the final outpost abandoned by Queen Titania's court when she led her subjects into exile, embittered by the changes in the World of Men; and my new home.

We made our way up into the foothills at the base of the tor, headed for a large opening in the foundation of the hill itself—the tunnel that would take us to the island of Ynis Witrin secreted within. A shiver ran down my spine as we approached, unsure as I was of what was in store. Would we experience a tangible presence of magic as we entered the hill? Encounter the lingering spirits of the heroes of old? Or perhaps catch a distant echo of the Wild Hunt?

As it turned out, the answer to all of these questions was a resounding no. When we crossed the tunnel's threshold, nothing at all happened, except we became slightly less wet. I glanced back over my shoulder, feeling strangely crestfallen.

"Is this all there is to it, then?" I said.

Nathaniel glanced at me in the thin light from the tunnel mouth, his lips quirking up at the corner.

"You expected a frenzied revel to pop into existence around us as soon as we crossed into the elfin lands?"

"No," I said quickly, despite my fancies in the preceding moments. Luckily, I had a change of subject close at hand. "But there are no guards, no defenses. What's to prevent the hill from being overrun?"

Nathaniel fished something out from beneath his collar. In the growing dark, I could just make out an amulet on a worn leather cord. It was a piece of grey stone roughly the size of his thumb, bound in silver wire.

"You've got to have one of these," he said. "It's a token that grants passage. Only those that are approved are able to get in."

"Couldn't somebody just purchase one if they had nefarious designs?" I said. "Or steal it?"

Nathaniel shook his head as he slipped the token back into his shirt. "The enchantment only works for the very person the token is crafted for. Well, and any of those that accompany them through the tunnel, such as your good self. You separate the token from the bearer, and it's just a chunk of rock."

I pondered this as we moved further into the tunnel and the light behind us diminished. I expected a corresponding illumination at the tunnel's far end to appear, but it remained elusive. Instead, the gloom became deeper and deeper, until the final glimmer from the Glastonbury side vanished, and we were in complete darkness.

You know, Esther, that the dark has never bothered me overmuch. It's why you would often come to my room in the night when we were children, seeking comfort after a bad dream or mysterious noise. But in that moment, I was struck with a painful awareness of the hill's weight suspended above us like the sword of Damocles, poised to collapse at any moment. I lost all sense of space and direction, trapped in a void with no up or down, no in or out, and felt a paralyzing stab of fear, but even worse was the all-consuming sense of hopelessness; I despaired of feeling anything like warmth or happiness ever again—only emptiness, until the end of time.

And then the light was back, getting closer and brighter with every beat of the horses' hooves. The awful panic, utterly debilitating in the moment, had passed. I breathed deeply, catching the faint odor of salt on the air, and glanced at Nathaniel, who seemed completely unaffected. Whether my trepidation had been merely an overpowering moment of disorientation or the result of some fairy spell, I could not say. But if it was the latter, I had indeed been mistaken about there not being defenses.

We reached the end of the tunnel quickly, emerging

into a sunny, if blustery, day. I had a fraction of a moment to contemplate the change in weather, but then I caught sight of the vista before us and gasped. While we had entered the tunnel at the base of the tor, now, somehow, we emerged on the crest of a grassy hill, and spread out below us was Ynis Witrin.

The road followed a gentle slope downward to an open sea. A narrow crescent of beach marked the transition from incline to flatland, then gave way to an expanse of mudflats, which, I am told, become fully submerged at high tide. Because the tide was out, I could see that there was a narrow, cobbled causeway running from the coast-line out to an island in the center of the flats. And atop that island stood the seat of the Seelie Court.

The outermost regions of the island are fairly level, at least until they reach a massive retaining wall surrounding a central peak. Structures spill down the surface of this peak in tiers, each with its own distinct character, creating an odd patchwork effect. At the summit, the castle, ancient and mysterious, seems almost to have grown from the rock itself, its lines liquid and mesmerizing in their beauty. Below that, perched on terraces bolstered by a combination of natural and manmade supports, sit clusters of buildings resembling many village centers across the English countryside, their design largely medieval and Tudor in nature. Meanwhile, outside the retaining wall, running along the shoreline, are streets lined with examples of architecture that could have been lifted whole cloth from elegant Georgian neighborhoods in London and deposited there near the sea.

We moved at a leisurely pace down the hill and onto the beach. I thought we might take the causeway, but instead, Nathaniel steered the horses out onto the flats, and we proceeded to make our way across the dense, damp sand. Gulls wheeled around us, but all else was quiet. I could almost imagine that we were the only inhabitants in this brave new world, whisked out of our everyday lives and consigned to a wholly solitary existence by some capricious fairy magic. For a moment, I thought I felt an echo of the crushing despondency I'd experienced in the tunnel, but as we got closer to the island, I detected some signs of life—figures hurrying about, smoke rising from chimneys to be caught in the breeze, and a flag bearing the crest of the Seelie Court waving at the foot of a dock that jutted out over the flats.

The dock was clearly meant to fulfill its traditional purpose for small craft while the tide was in, but it served our current needs well enough. As we approached, I noticed a handful of individuals waiting there, backs to the sky; two were dressed in army uniforms. The first, tall, dark, and powerfully built, stood at parade rest, spine ramrod straight and chin held high, while the other, slighter and fair, did not actually slouch but somehow gave the impression of doing so.

Nathaniel reined in the horses, bringing us even with a small ladder attached to the dock. The taller soldier stepped forward.

"Dr. Jarvis, I presume," he said, reaching down to help me out of the cart.

"Yes," I said, as I clambered onto the dock. "And you are"—I glanced at the insignia of rank on his jacket and recalled the name that had been on my correspondence from the embassy—"Captain Pryce?"

He gave me a sharp nod. "Nicholas Pryce of the 22nd Hussars. And this is Lieutenant Jacob Waddington of the 103rd Regiment, though we're all of the attaché's office while we're here on the island." Then, over his shoulder,

"Waddington, see to the baggage." Waddington glowered at us with bloodshot before deigning to comply.

"Usually, we give new arrivals some time to settle in," Pryce continued, extending a hand to usher me down the length of the dock and onto dry land, "but it's the delegation's allotted day for an audience with the queen, and she's actually on the island for once, so we should make a point of dropping in."

I raised my eyebrows. "Is it unusual for her to be in residence? Where else would she be?"

Pryce paused, giving me a startled look. "Why, the Home Lands, of course. You didn't think she *lived* here, did you?"

"I... Well, I suppose I never gave the matter much consideration."

Pryce shrugged. "In any case, she likes to at least lay eyes on new embassy staff."

"She does?" I couldn't imagine a low-level bureaucrat meriting that kind of attention from royalty.

Pryce nodded. "It's a very insular community here on the island. She prefers to keep her finger on the pulse." He glanced at me, and, noting my apprehension, continued. "Don't worry. It will be brief. I'll introduce you, you'll bow, and then we'll all go about our day. After that, I can show you around the British Quarter and take you by our office on the way to your quarters. Waddington will see about getting your things settled while we're out."

Waddington dropped one of my trunks on the dock with a resounding thud. "Is this truly the best use of my time today, Captain?"

"Yes, Lieutenant, it is," Pryce replied without a backward glance, though his eyes took on a look of long-suffering forbearance. "So, doctor, shall we go?"

"Er, certainly," I said, glancing around. "Will there be a conveyance, or will we be on foot?"

"No conveyance is nece—" He drew up short, catching sight of my worried look at the road that wound like some diabolical snake towards the island's summit, then gave a good-natured laugh. "Oh, no—we don't have to go that way. We'll take the stairs. Much more direct route." This didn't sound much less arduous to me, but I nodded and followed him towards the retaining wall.

"So, where do you hail from, doctor?" he asked. "Originally, I mean—you were obviously in London as of late."

"I was raised in Dorset, where my family still lives," I said, and he nodded.

"Not so far. Your people must be glad to have you close, especially after your time overseas."

I made an affirmative noise, choosing my next words carefully.

"My friends and family were somewhat... bewildered when I told them I was coming to live among the fae."

Pryce smiled wryly. "I imagine 'bewildered' is a generous description. My own mother begged me to reconsider when I told her."

It was a touch awkward to have my half-truth addressed so forthrightly, but there was some of comfort in it, too. Everyone knows Ynis Witrin is considered a backwater posting; I was relieved that Pryce, at least, was willing to dispense with any pretense to the contrary. As for the other members of the embassy delegation, it remained to be seen.

"Also," Pryce continued, "do not refer to them as 'fae'. I'm led to understand that they've never cared for it, but since Napoleon, it's fallen entirely out of favor—too French."

"It's been 70 years since Waterloo," I observed, and he shrugged.

"Their lives and memories are long. 'Elfin peoples' is acceptable, but they really prefer 'the Fair Folk' or, more often, just 'Folk' for short. "

We had reached the stairs built into the retaining wall, and as we mounted them, I paused to gaze out over the glistening water. "What's out there past the horizon?"

"Folk country," said Pryce, glancing back to make sure I was following.

"Is that the Home Lands you mentioned?" I asked, and he nodded. "What's it like? Out there?"

"I don't know," he said. "No humans do. The Folk are very tight-lipped about it."

I blinked. "But couldn't somebody just... sail out and check?"

"A few have tried," he said. "None have come back."

I might have thought he was toying with me, initiating the newest recruit with the specter of a macabre local legend, but his eyes remained steadily forward, and his voice was even He was entirely serious. I swallowed and hurried to keep pace with him as we reached the first tier of buildings.

As it happened, "the stairs" did not proceed in a straight line directly up the peak, like those of an ancient Mayan temple. Instead, short flights connected the terraces I'd seen from the flats, where offices, restaurants, and shops stood chock-a-block along the narrow streets. And what shops! All of them had been built on a scale to accommodate humans, or at least beings of comparable height, but each was alive with individuals of many sizes and shapes. Some creatures reached no higher than my waist and navigated the spaces via a cunningly contrived system of steps and handholds, while tiny figures with wings zipped through the air like so many maniacal butterflies.

And that's to say nothing of the goods on offer, which were articles of pure wonder. In a bakery window, I spotted what appeared to be a replica of the Hanging Gardens of Babylon created entirely of cake and spun sugar, its exquisite detail far beyond what any human craftsman could achieve. Another window boasted lamps, including some familiar models powered by oil, but also elegant glass structures containing soft light with no discernible source at all. An apothecary boasted an array of cosmetics housed in elaborate crystal bottles, the richly colored tinctures and oils swirling and shimmering in the sunlight. I could have stopped and lingered over any of them, but Pryce moved inexorably onward, providing a murmured commentary to me as we went.

"The ones that look most human are the elementals," he was saying. "There are four types, each with an affinity for a natural element: undines, sylphs, vulcani, and gnomes. You'll learn to distinguish them by appearance." He was correct in saying these looked the *most* human, for while they were roughly as tall as we were, their facial features and physiques, burly and fine-boned and of various statures in between, were nevertheless uncanny and, in some cases, almost eerie. "The smaller beings are brownies. They make up most of the laboring classes here. You'll want to stay on the good side of any who you come into contact with on a regular basis. They appreciate gifts of new clothes."

"And the flying ones?" I asked. He sighed deeply.

"Those are pixies. Do not, under any circumstances, give them clothing. They don't like it. Actually, there's not much they do like. It's really best to just avoid them if you can."

By then, we had neared an inner curtain wall that circled the castle. A pair of guards flanked a wrought-iron gate, and I noticed they looked different from the Folk we had seen on our way through the town—taller, with longer limbs and more angular features. They greeted Pryce with obvious recognition before shifting their exacting gazes to me.

"This is Dr. Jarvis," Pryce said by way of explanation. "New recruit. I'm here to escort him to the audience with Her Majesty." I found myself slightly taken aback by this address. I knew that it was correct, but it seemed odd to hear it in reference to anyone but Queen Victoria.

The guards nodded, and one gestured for us to enter the gate, but they watched us with a steady intensity I found disquieting. As we passed them, I realized where part of the feeling was coming from: they were the first semblance of a security force we had encountered on our tour. I mentioned this to Pryce.

"Well, the tunnel goes a long way towards keeping out bad actors," he said. "And the Folk are generally peaceable sorts. They tend to keep themselves to themselves."

"Even so, it feels strange for a place to have so little in the way of defense."

Pryce snorted. "Oh, the island is defended. The sentries are quite capable of neutralizing any threats."

I blinked. "I didn't see any sentries."

He chuckled softly. "Yes, that is rather the point."

"Those guards," I said, glancing over my shoulder. "Were they elementals?"

Pryce shook his head. "They were wights. Otherwise known as the courtly or the trooping Folk."

"I don't recall seeing any of them in the commercial district."

"No," Pryce said, with a bit on an edge to his tone.

"They rarely stray far from the castle. Honestly, they can be a bit high in the instep."

"Oh?"

"They make up most what passes for aristocracy here. The ruling class. And they don't let anyone forget it."

Pryce led us across the bailey to an arched doorway and into the castle proper. He moved with confidence, clearly having walked this route many times before, while I did my best not to gawk like a tourist. The halls buzzed with activity. There were even more brownies here than there had been in the commercial district, all moving with a brisk sense of purpose as they went about their duties. Elementals passed us in ones and twos, and I found I was already becoming able to distinguish them from one another. The gnomes were stocky, and most sported beards—including the women, though to a lesser extent than the men. The vulcani, meanwhile, were generally taller and more lavishly dressed, and they spoke passionately, emphasizing their points with broad hand gestures. The architecture, décor, and attire on display were all of a very distinctive style—the lines flowing and organic, the colors muted variations of green, brown, and yellow, with an occasional pop of lapis blue or primrose pink. The designs were beautiful, but a marked departure from the machine-made European textiles and furnishings I was used to. I also noticed that there were more than a few human servants present, which surprised me. I was going to ask Pryce about it, but I could see that we had reached our destination, so I filed it away for another time.

"Oh, one last thing," Pryce said, reaching for the door. "The Queen's Guard is composed entirely of women. Don't be alarmed when you see them. Or, at least, don't let on." And then we were in.

Compared to the pomp of anything associated with the

British court, the castle's throne room looked almost spare, though no less imposing. The space was vast and elegant, the floor of an almost silver marble veined in dark grey. Tall arched windows were framed in simply but beautifully worked stone, and the ceiling had been painted with an elaborate depiction of the celestial spheres. At the far end, backed by swags of cloth of gold, stood a dais where Queen Mab and her consort, Lord Owain, sat on austere thrones hewn from polished oak and upholstered in midnight blue velvet. Small groupings of courtiers flanked the royal couple, their expressions inscrutable. Railings along each side of the room formed galleries of sorts, where sumptuously dressed Folk lounged about, many drinking rich, dark wine from ornate goblets, though it was not yet noon.

As Pryce had said, a contingent of women was stationed at intervals around the perimeter of the room, with the most formidable positioned next to the dais. Her beautiful face was impassive, but her bearing suggested coiled power ready to strike. Her sistren followed her example, each standing at attention with a gleaming, beautifully wrought spear in her hand. But their weaponry was not the most noteworthy aspect of their martial raiment— they all wore trousers.

This was not the first time I had seen women appareled thus—in the East, women often wear trousers known as shalwars beneath coordinating tunics. But those garments are loose and flowing, doing almost as much to obscure the wearer's form as skirts. Such was not the case here. The guards were attired in leather armor, designed primarily for utility in combat, which meant it was fitted close to the body. The whole body. The effect was... distracting. I remembered Pryce's words and swallowed, hurrying to catch up with him as he went to stand by one of the railings.

In the center of the room, three human men sat at a table on chairs too spindly to accommodate them adequately. The heavily embellished, brightly colored furniture—which had presumably been provided by the castle staff and, admittedly, bore a striking resemblance to styles popular among the most patriotic Britons—looked almost comically garish compared to its surroundings. One of the men was outfitted in an army uniform, and I took him to be Colonel Abercrombie, my new commanding officer. The other two wore civilian attire and haughty expressions. These, I assumed, were the ambassador, Lord Cavendish, and secretary ambassador, Lord Marsden. I was not personally acquainted with either of them and wouldn't have been able to identify them by sight, but as Pryce and I took our place in the crowd, the larger of the two men was speaking directly to the queen, which suggested to me that he was the more senior.

The interaction did not seem to be going well.

"Your Majesty," Lord Cavendish said, spittle illuminated by a sunbeam. "As I have explained in the past, maintaining harmony between the major world powers is fundamental to the security and prosperity of Britain, and, by extension, the Seelie Court-"

"And as I have explained to *you*," the queen cut in, "It has become increasingly clear that Great Britain has grown less interested in halting foreign aggression to maintain a balance of power and more interested in expanding and establishing empire, which neither supports the interests of this court, nor merits the expenditure of our resources on Britain's behalf."

Lord Cavendish's face colored, and he mopped his brow with a handkerchief. In the gallery, one of the younger spectators, dandyish even in comparison to his associates, flicked a wrist in the direction of the table. There was a shiver in the air before him, then a sense of something shifting and turning, until a ghostly hand coalesced behind Cavendish's back.

"If I may, Your Majesty..." Lord Cavendish said and began rifling through the stack of papers on the table before him. As he did, the hand tapped him on the shoulder. At first, he did not acknowledge the touch, only twitched his muscles as if shaking off a fly. But then the hand tapped again, which distracted him enough that he lost his track of his shuffling and had to start over. The hand tapped a third time, and finally, Cavendish spun in his seat, only to find the space behind him empty, the hand having evaporated the instant he moved. Cavendish turned back to the throne with the same set-upon expression I'd seen on Pryce's face when talking to Waddington, while the prankster and his cohort buried their noses in their cups, sorting with laughter. Queen Mab looked unimpressed by every aspect of the scene.

One courtier standing near the queen leaned in to whisper something close to her ear. She listened intently, nodding, as we all looked on. A few of the Folk at the dais shifted restlessly, while others simply appeared bored, but one was noteworthy by virtue of his stillness and the cunning gleam in his eye as he scrutinized the exchange. Even to my untutored eye, the animosity of a political rivalry was clear.

Either oblivious or indifferent, the whispering courtier reached the end of his counsel and withdrew with a bow. The queen returned her full attention to Lord Cavendish.

"In the interest of the long-standing friendship between our nations," she said. "I will allow you time to prepare a document detailing the aims of Great Britain's foreign policy moving forward, in order to determine our position on the topic."

Lord Cavendish's eyes went steely. I knew men like him. They were used to being in charge and saw that authority as their birthright. For them, the notion of seeking anything like permission or approval for the measures taken by the Empire seemed beyond the pale. But constrained by his duty, he only nodded. "Thank you, Your Majesty."

"When we assisted you in the Crimea," she said, "it was to drive back the might of Imperial Russia. That was a worthy cause. Convince me that there is a similar one in play now."

Having just come from another military theater dictated by opposition to Russian interests, where the cause had ultimately seemed anything but worthy, I was taken aback by this statement. I did not have long to deliberate over it, however, because without another word, the queen snapped her attention away from the ambassador.

"Colonel Abercrombie," she said.

The colonel stood. "Yes, ma'am."

"I understand that there has been a recent addition to your staff. Is he here today?"

The colonel glanced over his shoulder, his eyes landing on Pryce. At his nod, Pryce stepped forward and bowed.

"Your Majesty," he said. "Please allow me to present Surgeon Wilfred Jarvis of the Army Medical Department."

Praying that I was not committing some obscure breach of etiquette, I took my place beside him and made my own bow. Upon standing, I was met with the penetrating stare of the queen of the Seelie Court.

Queen Mab could have been any age and no age at all. I could half believe she had sprung fully formed from the walls of the castle itself, like Athena from the head of Zeus, and it was easy to think of her as being just as legendary, a figure from a storybook. Sister and heir to the imperious Titania, it was she who had led the Folk back to the World of Men after two centuries of seclusion, she who had commanded the army that fought alongside British troops to defeat the French and halt Napoleon's drive across Europe. Only in our stories, she was portrayed almost as a mascot, a figurehead who served as a helpmeet to Wellington.

This woman was nobody's helpmeet.

"Welcome, doctor," she said, with just as much authority as she'd directed at Lord Cavendish, if slightly less opprobrium. "How do you find our humble island so far?"

"I've not gotten to see much of it yet, Your Majesty," I replied. "But it strikes me as a very fine place."

She smiled an elegant smile, one that communicated approval more than warmth. "I am happy to hear it. I understand that humans often do not know what to make of a place so... incongruous with that to which they are accustomed." She kept her eyes on me, but I sensed the words were not entirely for my benefit, an impression that was reinforced by the sound of an awkward throat-clearing coming from the ambassador's table.

"I am quite fascinated by the intricacies of human physiology," the queen continued pleasantly. "Perhaps you would be willing to discuss it with me in the future."

"As it pleases Your Majesty," I said. I worried that a full bow would be excessive, but I inclined my head in defer-ence. It seemed to be the right choice.

"Hmmm," she said and gave a serene nod. Apparently —thankfully—I had passed muster. Without another word to me, she returned her focus to Lord Cavendish.

"This audience is concluded. We will reconvene in a

fortnight, at which time I expect to see the report I have requested."

Lord Cavendish responded with something approximating a nod, clearly ready to be done with the interaction. It was a notably discourteous display, and the queen's eyebrows went up ever so slightly.

"Am I to understand, sir, that this arrangement does not meet with your approval? Have the workings of this court somehow offended your delicate sensibilities?"

"No, Your Majesty," Lord Cavendish said, his voice tight. I was reminded of a common bit of whispered speculation regarding the Folk—that they are able to see through lies—and wondered if it was true.

But if Mab recognized the falsehood, and I couldn't see how she wouldn't, she gave no indication. only nodded again and rose to her feet, Lord Owain following close behind. However irreverent the assembled Folk may have appeared the moment before, now every subject dropped into a bow or curtsy. One of the armored women opened a cunningly concealed door near the dais, and the royal couple swept through it. As soon as the door closed behind them, conversation resumed, and in short order, fresh cups of wine were passed around.

Lord Cavendish, Lord Marsden, and Colonel Abercrombie huddled together near the table, talking amongst themselves. I thought perhaps we would join them, but Pryce tugged at my sleeve.

"Come on. I'll take you to the office, and the colonel will join us there later."

We retraced our steps through the castle corridors, and soon we were navigating the steps of the commercial district in reverse. The spectacle was still captivating, but having seen it once, I was able to devote more attention to conversation.

"How did all of you come to be here?" I said. "In the attaché's office, I mean."

"Colonel Abercrombie was about to retire when he was asked to take the position by the Foreign Secretary," Pryce replied. "I was already serving under him at the time, and he invited me to come along."

I cast Pryce a sidelong glance. He gave every indication of being an exemplary officer; such an acceptance made little sense. "You came here rather than seeking advancement in the infantry?"

He pressed his lips into a grim line. "My father served in the Punjab with the East India Company before the Mutiny in '57. That's where my mother is from. It turns out many soldiers don't like the idea of taking orders from a half-caste."

"Ah," was all I could think to say to that.

"Father would have preferred that none of us followed him into the military," Pryce continued. "But he only has one heir. The rest of us had to do something for a living."

"You're a second son?" I guessed.

"Third," Pryce said bemusedly. "Our middle brother decided to pursue law. He offered to set me up in his firm, but I couldn't picture myself as a solicitor—cooped up in offices and courtrooms for months at a stretch."

I nodded, recognizing a kindred spirit in this respect. "And Waddington?"

Here, Pryce rolled his eyes. "Waddington is 'on loan' from his regiment."

I considered this. "I don't believe I am familiar with that practice."

"It means someone wanted to be rid of Waddington but didn't want to stir up a scandal with an ignominious discharge, and so, thanks to Waddington's family connections, he ended up here."

Eventually, we came back around to the dock, which constituted something of a midpoint in the milieu at the base of the island. Stretching out to either side and wrapping around the retaining wall were the newer buildings I had noticed earlier. A quick glance told me there were far fewer Folk down here; almost everyone I saw was human.

"Everything down here is referred to as the British Quarter," Pryce said. "The businesses and common buildings are closest to the center, and then it becomes residences out toward either end. Down there—" he gestured to the right— "you have support services and the like. School, chapel, lending library, commissary, assembly rooms, etc. The official buildings are down this way." He lifted his chin to the left and began leading me down a central thoroughfare in that direction.

As we went, he highlighted points of interest—the post office, supply depot, ambassador's residence and so on. At length, we came to a series of nearly identical buildings devoted to offices, and Pryce explained to me which departments resided in each.

"And this one is ours," he said as we reached the last one. He stepped up to the door, opened it with a key from his jacket pocket, and led us into the dark interior.

"Waddington!" he called out, but only received silence in reply. I could hear him cursing the man under his breath as he set about turning up the lamps and I took in my surroundings. The reception area was modest but pleasant, paneled in a rich, polished wood and graced with elegant flourishes. A railing with a swinging door in the center ran the length of the room, dividing the initial entry from a larger area boasting a pair of desks that faced each other, plants in brass buckets, and a Union Jack on a pole in the corner.

"Is this a space for clerks?" I asked. "Or secretaries?"

"At present, neither," Pryce said. "Waddington and I take turns working the front desk and completing basic office duties; you'll be added to the rota."

I nodded. Through our correspondence, I had come to understand that while the embassy community needed a doctor—many are leery of Folk healing, and visiting Glastonbury for a medical concern was often less than ideal—I would also be contributing to the administration of the attaché's office. I did not know precisely what my contributions would be, but I figured all would be revealed in time. My head was already spinning from all I'd encountered, so I was disinclined to press the issue.

From the entry, Pryce led me through a door into a long hallway, which boasted a handful of private offices for staff members and a larger, better appointed one for the colonel. My own office was at the far end on the left. It was not much to speak of—really just an alcove with a plain desk and chair—but it would do. As we made our way back to the reception area, the colonel himself arrived.

He's not a large man, Colonel Abercrombie, but he carries himself with elan and gives an overall sense of capability. He has the weathered skin of a man who has spent many years campaigning in the sun and a rather magnificent set of white mustaches. I liked him at once.

"Happy to meet you, Jarvis," he said as he shook my hand. "It will be good to have some fresh blood around the place."

"I'm happy to be here, sir."

"You did well in the audience. The queen is an intimidating woman, but you handled yourself with aplomb."

"Thank you, sir. Are audiences normally quite so…"

"Perilous?" the colonel offered. "Agonizing?"

"'Fraught' was more what I had in mind."

"Ah," he said with a grin, clapping me on the shoulder

—the good one, thankfully. "I can see why they sent you—a diplomat at heart."

"Yes, sir."

"Fine, fine," he said, then shifted his attention to Pryce. "I have those reports to look over, captain. I'll be in my office."

"Yes, sir," Pryce said. As the colonel left the room, he beckoned me over to the desk, where he had collected a variety of items.

"I put together some documents to help you get acclimated," he said handing me a thick file folder. "Look over them at your leisure. Here's your house key, office key, and the token that will allow you to circulate between the island and Glastonbury." I accepted all of these, lingering on the wire-wrapped stone that was similar to Nathaniel's, though it had not been strung on a cord. I turned it over slowly in my hand, recalling the misery of the tunnel with some apprehension. Pryce took note of my contemplation, lifting his chin at the token.

"Don't lose that unless you want to cause an international incident."

I looked at him sharply, unable to tell if this was hyperbole. His face remained unmoved, however, and I carefully tucked the token into the inside pocket of my uniform jacket.

"Now," he said. "How would you like to see your new home?"

I was prepared for another lengthy walk, but when we stepped outside, Pryce led me to a cluster of plain but tidy houses separated from the office by only a wide lawn. We stopped before a cottage with a pebbled front walk and petunias in the front window boxes, and I tapped the plaque bolted to the front door.

"221B?"

Pryce nodded. "I'm in 221A, and Waddington is 221C." He gestured first to the left and then to the right. "The colonel's house is the plain, unadorned 221, just down there. His staff can help with your cooking and cleaning, if you like, until you are able to hire your own housekeeper."

"I don't think that will be necessary," I said. "I'm used to doing for myself."

He nodded in understanding—he was a soldier, too, after all.

"Well, then," he said. "Take the rest of the day to get settled. We'll see you in the morning."

I nodded and watched him go. Then I came inside, looked around at my unpacked baggage, which had been left strewn haphazardly across the living area, and promptly took out this diary. Now that I have recorded the day for posterity, I plan to find some supper and go over the documents Pryce gave me. After that, I may call it an early night; I had hoped to get some reading in, but I am quite tired, and I can feel the beginnings of a dull throb in my shoulder. The trunks will keep.

Your brother,
Wilf

Chapter 6

13 March 1881

DEAR ESTHER,

One of the most confounding things about living in Ynis Witrin is how a place where actual magic exists can feel so… provincial.

I realized very quickly that the members of the embassy community do not readily fraternize with either the Folk or the local humans who work and make their homes on the island. Rather, they have created a facsimile of English society in miniature. For example, the ladies have developed a distinct and quite rigid set of rules for visiting and card-leaving, the intricacies of which escape me. There is no shortage of events in the evening, from private suppers to receptions hosted by Mrs. Cavendish in the ambassador's residence, but unlike in larger cities and towns, where the company is varied, all of these occasions are attended by the same handful of guests. A strict social hierarchy is observed among those guests, within which I, as the most junior member of the attaché staff, rank at the bottom. There is no Hyde Park to promenade in, but otherwise, life amongst the Britons here seems to proceed much as it would in society outside the tor.

This attitude of exclusivity extends even to questions of health. I was looking forward to putting my professional expertise to use far from the battlefield, but in truth, there is no real need for me here. The vast majority of complaints that I have been called upon to address could easily have been dealt with by a midwife or apothecary, both of which are available on the island. It is only that many of the embassy staff and their families—landed gentry and wealthy commoners alike—feel entitled to a proper healer, a human healer, one educated at a storied university. Even the fact that I bear the title of "surgeon" rather than the more-prestigious "physician" is of no consequence. I am respectable, and I am at their beck and call. That is enough.

This is but one example of how, increasingly, I find myself at odds with my associates on an almost existential level. Oh, I manage all right with my own staff—even Waddington isn't able to flout all notions army discipline and rigor—but the civilians seem increasingly foreign to me. I have thought many, many times of Father and his admonitions against the wealth and status prized by the noble classes. However we used to laugh about his diatribes, I am discovering that he was right about the insidious allure of prestige, as he was about so many things.

The most recent, and perhaps most representative, of these instances occurred last night when I was dining at the Cavendish residence. A representative of the attaché's office is expected at all social gatherings, and we take them in turns so none of us need shoulder an unreasonable burden. As usual, the meal was extravagant, almost indecently so, considering the frequency with which such affairs are conducted here. I found myself woolgathering, musing on Our Lord's teachings regarding the poor in Luke as conversation hummed around me, when I was startled by someone calling my name down the table.

"Dr. Jarvis," Lord Cavendish said. "You are a man of science. I presume you are familiar with the work of Mr. Darwin?"

"Yes, my lord," I said, wiping my mouth with a napkin and striving to maintain an air of deference in the face of such an inane question.

"What do you think of this theory of polygenesis I keep hearing about?"

I furrowed my brow. "Polygenesis, my lord?" For while I of course know of polygenesis, I could not fathom his motivation in bringing it up.

He settled back in his chair, sipping his wine. "Yes. Lately, I've come across some interesting ideas about the evolutionary past of the Folk. We tend to consider them collectively as one body, thanks to their affinity for magic, but apparently, some scholars are coming to believe that the various types have descended from different ancestors and that, furthermore, they may be more closely related to peoples of our own world than they are to each other."

I have also heard murmurings of this sort from time to time, but dismissed them as pseudoscientific bunk. It was tempting to say so to Lord Cavendish, but that would have been a scandalous breach of etiquette, and I hoped to steer clear of anything that might expose the attaché's office to censure. I cleared my throat. "Very interesting, my lord.

Do you believe there to be any practical utility attached to such speculation?"

He snorted. "I don't know about utility, but it does help one understand the workings of things. For example, it would make sense for us and the wights to have a close connection. We are similar in appearance and temperament; we have a common appreciation of order and penchant for civilization. But what about the brownies? With their diminutive size and subservient nature, they seem more analogous to the pygmies of Uganda and Morocco than enlightened peoples."

"What about the elementals?" said Lord Marsden. "Within which category would they fall?"

"Neither," said Lord Cavendish. "Some speculate they metamorphosed from the spirits of the very earth, air, fire, and water themselves. Sounds daft to me, but then, I suppose innovations in the sciences often do, until they become widely accepted."

"And what of the pixies, dear?" Lady Cavendish said, sounding bored. "Where might they have come from?"

"I have heard it said that they are related to insects," interjected Lady Marsden. She looked to Lord Cavendish. "Would such a thing be possible?"

Her husband gave a dry laugh. "They would be the poor cousins, surely. Insects at least contribute something to the world—producing honey, for example, or silk. Pixies are, well… pixies."

Many around the table, including Lord Cavendish, gave knowing chuckles. When the sounds of mirth subsided, the ambassador returned his attention to me.

"But we have strayed from my original question. What do you think, doctor, as a medical man?"

I took a sip of wine to buy myself a moment. Even taking into account my experiences on the island up to that point, I was taken aback by the casual disdain Lord Cavendish showed for the Folk, to say nothing of the African peoples he had mentioned. This man was a representative of Her Majesty's government, sent to treat with the Folk, and yet he seemed to feel no compunction about speaking of them in such a disparaging manner. No wonder they showed him such open contempt. His persistence was somewhat understandable, though, if nobody in his retinue saw fit to voice a different opinion. I did see fit, but I knew I had to tread carefully, so I sought to temper my words.

"Whoever their ancestors, they are all endowed with worth and dignity by their Creator. That fundamental truth should take precedence over any other distinctions devised by men, wouldn't you agree, my lord?"

I managed to keep my tone cool and even, so much so that at first, Lord Cavendish didn't seem to take my meaning. But then I saw a flicker of understanding in his eyes, and his face darkened.

Lady Cavendish might have noticed this as well because she said, "Oh, yes, doctor, of course you are right. Dearest, how are you enjoying your lamb?" and I was spared a dressing down in favor of Lord Cavendish waxing poetic about his dinner. We continued eating, and nobody else addressed me while we were at the table.

When the meal was over, I made my excuses and departed before the men retired for cigars and brandy. I cannot regret my actions, but I wonder if this encounter may have ramifications for me down the line. Indeed, if I had anywhere else to go that held more promise, I would be hard pressed to stay here any longer. I fear, however, that if I returned to England, I would still be consumed by this confounded ennui, on top of which the forfeiture of my position here would be documented on my military record, and who knows what that would mean for my future prospects. So I suppose I shall do my best to brazen it out. Perhaps things will improve, or failing that, I will become inured to them and able to content myself with brandy and cigars. How grim.

Your dejected brother,

Wilf

Chapter 7

20 March 1881

DEAR ESTHER,

I have not been able to bring myself to write over the past week, consumed by the jaded sentiments I described in my last entry and weary of the day-to-day monotony. Tonight, however, my melancholy was disrupted by something entirely unprecedented.

Tomorrow is the spring equinox, which many of the Folk celebrate as a holiday called Ostara. In honor of the observance, Lord and Lady Cavendish hosted a ball, to which, counter to their usual habit, they invited representatives from the castle. It was held in the Quarter's assembly rooms rather than the ambassador's residence and was an even more opulent affair than usual.

While ostensibly intended to honor the beliefs and traditions of the Folk, the event was in truth an excuse to show off the glory of the Empire. This began with the choices of decor and music. While the Folk are master craftsmen, using magic—or, as they call it, "glamour"—to achieve dizzying feats of beauty and grace, they are quite literal-minded, drawing almost entirely from what can be perceived with the senses. Also, while we humans are only able to detect the outward manifestations of this glamour, they can see the underpinnings at work, which robs the efforts of the same delight and wonder which they inspire in us. Thus, many of their kind are fascinated by the way human art utilizes imagination, that unique ability of our most creative minds to innovate and conjure up fancies from nothing. As such, the improvised ballroom was awash with human ingenuity.

The walls of the room had been adorned with panels of silk depicting famous scenes from Shakespeare—the madness of Ophelia, Brutus's betrayal of Caesar, Henry V delivering his St. Crispin's Day speech—and a depiction of the Globe Theatre had been chalked on the dancefloor, impressive even as its lines became scuffed and blurred underfoot. (It did not escape my notice that there were no references to the Bard's portrayals of the Folk, and certainly not to Mercutio's speech diminishing Mab to a mere pixie, however tempting such a slight must have been for our host.) A string quartet sat in a corner, playing the type of music that was popular in London drawing rooms rather than the music favored by the Folk, which is inspired by birdsong and running water and leans heavily on harp and flute.

Even the refreshments table made a statement. Next to steaming samovars of tea and coffee sat a bowl of punch fortified with Jamaican rum. Platters boasted pasties flavored with Caribbean peppers, fragrant Indian samosas, and a panoply of confections featuring coconuts, pineapples, and other fruits from around the Empire. The vast majority also boasted refined sugar, which the Folk rarely eat. It was an overt display of wealth and influence that, ironically, left me with no appetite whatsoever.

If the Folk in attendance were troubled by similar sentiments, though, I could not tell, and some of them were of a type would seem predisposed to such attitudes. I have learned that the Folk closest to the queen, and on the island at large really, fall into two main camps: the isolationists, who wish for the queen to break diplomatic ties with us and take the Folk back into the Home Lands, and the pro-alliance faction, who hope to maintain and even strengthen relations. A surprising number of isolationists had accepted their invitations to the event, and their leader, a Lord Evrain—who I now recognized as the particularly dour courtier from my first audience with the queen—was circulating through the crowd, seeming civil enough—charming even. He was smiling whenever I caught sight of him, with his subordinates trailing along behind him in submissive obeisance. Indeed, a general feeling of amity pervaded the room, a willingness to let differences go and simply have a pleasant time.

For my own part, I had thought myself resigned to dancing with the requisite number of ladies that would allow me to slip away without eliciting accusations of incivility. After only two waltzes and a polka, however, I felt stifled and agitated, thinking longingly of my peaceful cottage and the unfinished book on my nightstand. Just as I began to believe I might actually expire from the tedium, the musicians—wonderfully, mercifully—called for a break, and I retreated hastily to the terrace for some air.

The night was deliciously cool, coming as I had from the stuffy confines of the ballroom, but also nearly bright as day. The pergola that arched over the terrace had been laden with hundreds of candles; in keeping with the tone of the night, any glamoured sources of light had been banished in favor of good old beeswax, danger of setting the entire place ablaze be damned. I couldn't help shaking my head at the pomposity. But that was just the way of this whole endeavor, I mused. I had believed my posting to Ynis Witrin to be a new start, but ultimately, my pursuits on the island were proving ever more preposterous and foolish. I felt rather like a child who'd been offered a tasty pudding, only for it to be snatched away.

I sighed and felt a twinge in my shoulder, likely a result of the dancing. I extended my left arm and, gripping the shoulder with my right hand, twisted gently, attempting to ease the stiffness along my back and neck. After a moment, I felt some relief, and, releasing my hold, was attempting to cajole myself back inside, but then—

"You have been in Afghanistan, I perceive," a low feminine voice said out of the shadows.

I turned in its direction. "Beg pardon?"

The figure who emerged from the gloom was tall by human standards, though not of a stature with most courtly Folk. Her face had the look of that group in the sharpness of her cheekbones and the line of her nose, but that harsh angularity was softened by a curving cheek and full lower lip. Her eyes were wide and tilted at the corners, a shining grey that called to mind the sea before a storm, and pale blonde hair was piled in curls atop her head. She was dressed in an ice blue gown heavy with silver embroidery in that elemental style I was coming to associate with Mab's court, while at her throat she wore the sculptural figure of a snake consuming its tail, a common sight in London society inspired by Queen Victoria's own tastes. She was an odd amalgamation of my old world and my new one.

"Afghanistan," she repeated. "You have been there recently, if I am not mistaken."

"I have," I said, mystified. "But how could you possibly have known that?"

She tapped her chest, just over her heart, and inclined her head in my direction. "Army Medical Department. 66th Regiment of Foot, isn't it?"

I nodded, looking down at my own chest where my service medal gleamed in the candlelight.

"I wasn't *quite* sure I was remembering accurately," she continued. "I've read reports of the Battle of Maiwand, but the papers we receive here are often woefully out of date, which makes it difficult to keep my thinking as orderly as I'd like. However, I noted your wrists are paler than the rest of your skin, indicating time spent in the sun, likely in a tropical clime. You also hold yourself with military bearing, but with the stiffness of pain. Were you injured in action?"

I nodded, still feeling vaguely thunderstruck. "Took a bullet to the shoulder."

Her eyes brightened with interest. "Ah! Were the bones affected? Perhaps muscular or arterial damage? Did you experience any infection in the wound? No, I suppose you wouldn't have or you'd no longer be with us, medical conditions on the battlefield being what they are. Dr. Lister's ideas on germ theory have made happy inroads, but it must be difficult to maintain a strict system of antisepsis while on the march."

I was left scrambling for a response to this dissertation, but just then, music drifted through the open terrace doors, the players apparently restored by application of refreshment. The lady turned her head in its direction with a soft "Oh!'. Lifting her chin, her eyes fluttered closed.

"Brahms," she said, more to herself than to me. "The String Quartet No.1—"

"In C Minor" I finished, and she opened her eyes, gifting me with a dazzling smile.

"You know his work?"

"I do," I said. "Though my sister is the real musician in the family."

"Oh, but Brahms really is lovely, don't you think?" She did not wait for a response. "I know he is regarded as conservative compared to the New German School, but he exhibits a profound understanding of form, and I find his use of counterpoint particularly satisfying, A composition does not need to be swamped in angst, after all, to be meaningful." She gave a contented sigh, turning her full attention to the music once more.

As we stood there together, listening in amiable silence, a dark-skinned woman dressed in black with a pristine white apron and lace cap, hurried through the open doors. She had a look of grave intent on her face, but she faltered at the sight of me.

"Oh! Excuse me, sir," she said in the lilting tones of the West Indies and bobbed a quick curtsy. "I didn't realize you were here"

I was opening my mouth to dismiss her concerns, but my companion was quicker.

"What is it, Mary?" she said, a new note of alertness in her voice. With a wary glance at me, Mary crossed the terrace and leaned in close to her mistress's ear, speaking urgently but also softly enough that I could not overhear her words. As the lady listened, her face became drawn and serious, and when she lifted her gaze to me once more, her eyes were grim.

"I must go," she said with a brisk nod of her head. "Deepest apologies—it really has been a pleasure speaking with you."

And without another word she hurried back into the ballroom with the maid and vanished into the crowd.

I could only stand there blinking after her for a stunned moment. Then, almost by instinct, I dove after her.

As I pushed through the throng, I cast my gaze about to the left and right, straining my eyes for a glimpse of pale curls and ice blue silk, but to no avail. It was as if my mysterious companion had simply evanesced like an elusive dream, which, I realized, was entirely possible, assuming she had even been real and not some glamour-induced vision.

I came to a section of the room where the press of bodies had abated somewhat and was giving the space one last sweeping look when I realized someone had come up beside me.

"Jarvis," Pryce's voice said, and I gave him a grunt of acknowledgement, not taking my eyes off the revelers.

"Jarvis, we need to go. Now."

This time, I caught a note of urgency in his voice, something I couldn't recall hearing from him since I'd arrived on the island. Finally, I abandoned my hunt and turned to look at him.

"What is it?"

He pursed his lips. "There's been a murder."

Chapter 8

20 March 1881, cont.

IN A RUSH, we retrieved our hats and abandoned the ball, forgoing even perfunctory farewells. To my surprise, when we reached the high street, we did not turn in the direction of the crowded commercial district and the castle, but instead toward the far end of the Quarter which is composed entirely of residences. I'd yet to have a reason to venture out much further than the office complex, so there were many areas toward the edge of the settlement that I had never seen. It felt strange making my first foray into these environs in the dark.

Also, the night was unnervingly still. Pryce and I were the only souls out on the street, our footsteps echoing against the cobbles. This seemed at odds with the magnitude of our errand, and I glanced back at the assembly hall to see if anyone was following us, but all was quiet.

"I'd've thought a development like this would cause more of a stir," I mused to Pryce.

"It's not common knowledge yet. Word will spread soon enough, but the Ynis Witrin Constabulary sought me out specifically because the victim was a soldier, so we have a bit of a head start."

I cast a sideways glance at him. "Ynis Witrin has its own constabulary?"

"It's a glorified night watch," he said. "Any serious infractions among the Folk are dealt with at the castle, the embassy handles anything involving staff or their families, and the human servants fall under the jurisdiction of the Glastonbury authorities."

I blinked. "What, even the ones that live on the island?"

Pryce shrugged. "That wasn't a consideration back when these things were being decided."

"Well, if the constabulary has no real authority, what's the point of them?"

Pryce sighed. "You must be aware by now that Lord Cavendish is not what you'd call popular among the Folk."

I nodded. "I had noticed that, yes."

"Some of it is not his fault," Pryce continued. "His predecessor, Lord Warburton, was a favorite of the queen's and was highly respected—beloved, even—by most of the Folk on the island. It was an arrangement that suited everybody, and from what I've gathered, Warburton hated to leave the post, but his health was deteriorating, and his family insisted that he retire to the country for his final years. Stepping into his role would have been difficult for anyone, but Lord Cavendish..." He trailed off without explaining what he meant, but he didn't have to. I knew.

"When he arrived, and Folk and humans alike realized how ill-equipped he was for the job, it threw the island into turmoil. Cavendish was forced to make some changes and concessions to keep the various factions happy. Forming the constabulary was one of those olive branches, to help assuage fears that the embassy staff would go feral and wreak havoc without a strong leader at the head. That's also largely the reason Colonel Abercrombie was asked to take the military attaché position; the Foreign Secretary wanted someone here who knew what they were doing." I decided it must be the solitude that was making Pryce so forthcoming; very little of what he said surprised me, but he rarely shared his opinions so explicitly. "Anyway, the chaos never materialized, of course, so now the constables mostly just wander around in uniforms feeling overly important. The chief is a good man, though, so that's something."

Throughout this conversation, our steps had never slowed, and by this time, we had almost reached the end of the high street. "Where precisely are we going, by the way?" I said.

"The crime occurred in one of the new cottages being constructed on the edge of the Quarter."

I raised my eyebrows. "New cottages? For whom?" It was hardly as if there were ravening throngs clamoring to move to Ynis Witrin.

"They're for the human workers from town," Pryce replied. "So they don't have to travel back and forth every day."

Turning off of the main road, we entered an unpaved lane lined with the shells of semi-detached cottages. Our path was dark, the buildings reduced to indistinct shapes, but about halfway down the row, a dull glow emanated from a window. This, evidently, was our destination.

When we reached the cottage, a few men in helmets and dark wool capes, presumably the inconsequential constables, were milling about outside, speaking in low voices. The exterior doors of the dwelling had not yet been installed; instead, the empty thresholds were draped with canvas to keep out the elements, as were the vacant windows. Pryce nudged aside the swath of canvas serving as the front door, and we stepped inside. The glow I had noticed came from a handful of lanterns that had been placed around the room, casting strange, angular shadows.

The chamber was plain, but serviceable. In shape, it was a simple rectangle with an interior doorway opening onto a dark space that was likely the kitchen and a set of stairs leading to the upper floor. It had that particular air of promise that new places do, with traces of sawdust on the floor and fresh whitewash on the walls, but that feeling was spoiled by the contorted body in the center of the room. The surrounding area was lurid with blood, its metallic tang threatening to overpower the scents of cut wood and paint. Perhaps most chillingly, someone had used some of the blood to write "SAIS" on the wall next to the fireplace.

"What is that?" I murmured to Pryce, gesturing to the writing. "'Sais'?"

"It's Welsh for 'Englishman'," Pryce replied. "Some of the Folk use it as a general term of derision for anyone they see as an outsider."

Just then, a constable approached us, nodding at Pryce. "Captain."

"Chief Constable," Pryce returned, and they shook hands. "This is Dr. Jarvis. Jarvis, this is Chief Constable Charles Lester." Lester extended his hand to me, and I shook it.

"What exactly are we looking at?" Pryce continued.

"Alarm went up about an hour ago," Lester said. "We had to send word to the castle, but I thought you'd want a look, too, before we moved the body. We need to get on top of this, or the place will be a circus when word gets out."

Pryce nodded and looked down at the body. "Any iden-
tification?"

The Chief constable shook his head. "No. Just the
uniform. Didn't think he was one of your people, but since
he was army…"

"Yes, thank you for alerting us," Pryce said. "Fore-
warned is forearmed. Even if he isn't officially one of ours,
he came to be here somehow, and we're liable to get
dragged into the middle of it."

As Pryce finished his statement, the canvas over the
door was swept aside, and one of the courtly Folk entered.
With a jolt, I realized that I recognized him. He was the
one who I had seen whispering in Mab's ear on my first
day in Ynis Witrin—the one seemingly at odds with Lord
Evrain. He was short for a wight, and broader through the
chest and shoulders than was typical, which, coupled with
his neat, trim beard, gave him an almost gnomish look. It is
always tricky to figure the age of the Folk, but I would have
guessed this one to be somewhere in his late middle years.
His eyes were bright but lined at the corners, and there
were strands of silver in the dark hair that curled up from
his forehead.

Lester and Pryce both inclined their heads to the
newcomer, who nodded in return. Turning to me, Pryce
said "Dr. Wilfred Jarvis, may I introduce Sir Robin
Goodfellow."

My first instinct was to roll my eyes and chide Pryce for
such an obvious and amateur jest, but again, I was recalled
to awareness of my present circumstances.

"Oh!" I stammered. "You mean, *the* Robin
Goodfellow?"

Next to me, I saw Pryce wince as Robin Goodfellow's
face took on a look of deep bemusement.

"The very same," he said, in the weary fashion of

someone who had already had this conversation more times than he would have liked.

"Please forgive my lack of decorum," I said. "I meant no offense. I was just… caught off guard."

"It's all right," he said. "Master Shakespeare is really to blame, with his liberal use of creative license. He created a set of expectations I am perpetually unable to meet."

His words were wry, but his eyes were warm, so it seemed he did not hold a grudge. I gave him a tentative smile, and he looked to Lester.

"Thank you for sending word. I apologize for the delay, but we were engaged."

"We?" Pryce said. "Who else is—"

Just then, the canvas was again thrown back, and to my great shock, a woman strode into the room.

"Chief Constable, honestly!!" she said, pointing behind her to the path outside. "If a herd of buffaloes had passed along there, it could not have created a greater mess— Oh!" She gasped, drawing up short. "It's you!"

It was the lady I had met at the ball. She had changed, trading her elaborate gown for a pair of tan trousers, a linen shirt, and shining leather boots, and she had a canvas bag slung across her torso, but her hair was still arranged for the ball, elegant curls trailing along the length of her neck and over her shoulder. I could only stare at her in wordless astonishment.

Pryce glanced back and forth between us. "Have the two of you already been acquainted?"

"Not formally—" I began, but the lady seemed content to dispense with pleasantries, stepping forward and extending her hand to me, rather as if she were a man.

"Miss Honoria Sherwood, at your service," she said. Something about the name niggled at my memory, but I couldn't quite place it, distracted as I was by her proffered hand. Nonplussed, I took it, noting that her grip was confident and firm. "And you are?"

"Dr. Wilfred Jarvis," I replied and gave a quick bow out of habit, though it was rather superfluous following the handshake.

"Lately of the 66th Regiment," she said with a smile. I fumbled for a response, but was rescued by Goodfellow calling the lady's name and drawing her away.

Pryce took a step closer to me.

"You didn't tell me you knew Miss Sherwood," he murmured.

"I don't," I replied. "Or rather, I didn't, until this evening. Why is that noteworthy? Who is she?"

"She's something of an anomaly in Ynis Witrin, along with her sister," Pryce said. "Their lineage is rather out of the ordinary—quite scandal, as I am told."

"Oh? How so?"

"Her mother is General Caelia, captain of the Queen's Guard."

"Well, that explains the trousers," I murmured, remembering the formidable woman in the throne room. Pryce made a vague affirmative sound.

"And her father?" I said.

"Sir Arthur Sherwood, the baronet and explorer."

I understood then why the name had seemed familiar. Sir Arthur had been such a romantic, infamous figure in our childhood. We'd all heard the story of the brilliant and endlessly curious son of a marquess, one of the youngest students ever to matriculate from Oxford, but notorious for his outlandish antics and stunts. We knew that when those stunts had become too much for polite society to stomach, his disgusted father had disowned him, and he had gone to sea. Then there were the years spent traveling in South America, the writings published back in Britain to wide acclaim, and the return home to a hero's welcome and restoration to respectability when Queen Victoria created him a baronet, owing to his contributions to the field of natural history and anthropology.

And there was the Folk wife.

I had always thought it neatly done, the way the couple had sidestepped the ensuing controversy by disappearing entirely. They slipped out of society with nary a whisper, and without any public developments to fuel it, the gossip about them had died down. Society had moved onto other peccadilloes, and the fate of the dashing swashbuckler and his fairy bride remained a quixotic mystery.

One that I had now apparently solved.

"What is her connection to Goodfellow?" I asked.

"He is one of the queen's closest advisers, and he reportedly thinks highly of Miss Sherwood's character and intellect. He has taken her under his wing, made her something of a protégé."

"But she's barely more than a girl," I protested.

Pryce shrugged. "Age works differently for the Folk. Plus, she's out in society back in England. I suppose if she is eligible for marriage, she is eligible for…" He gestured vaguely in the lady's direction. "Whatever that is."

As we spoke, she had been moving slowly around the room, her sharp eyes scanning its confines. When she reached the grisly writing on the wall, she slipped a hand into her bag and withdrew a large magnifying glass, which she proceeded to use in a close examination of the spoiled whitewash. Apparently satisfied, she returned the glass to her bag, replacing it with a small notebook and a dressmaker's tape. Then she dropped to her knees and began taking measurements of the floor that, to my eye, seemed completely arbitrary, all while muttering to herself and jotting things down in the notebook.

"Were you able to determine anything regarding the cause of death?" Pryce asked Lester, who shook his head.

"We've no idea, captain. I was rather hoping you could help us out with that bit."

"No idea?!" I burst out, surprising even myself. I couldn't help it; his words had pricked at my occupational pride. "With that amount of blood, I would think the source would be obvious."

Again, Lester shook his head. "It's not his blood, sir. The man doesn't have a mark on him."

"Not his blood?" I repeated. Across the room, Miss Sherwood paused in the act of sweeping a grainy substance into a small paper envelope and sat back on her heels.

"He is entirely correct, doctor," she said. "The body bears no discernible wounds. But perhaps you would like to take a look yourself?"

I did not miss the note of challenge in her voice, and while a better man might have been able to dismiss it, I could not. Swallowing, I stepped forward and crouched next to the body, taking in the most notable details of its current state. The man was, I suppose, what some would call handsome, with full, dark hair thick with pomade and a carefully waxed mustache. There was some bruising on his face, with notable swelling around the nose, but even so, he seemed oddly peaceful, as if he had simply laid down to sleep, wholly insensible of the surrounding carnage. Perplexed, I conducted a cursory examination and discovered that Miss Sherwood and the constable had been correct—the victim's head and hands were completely intact, and wherever the uniform bore traces of blood, it was easy to see that the substance had been splashed onto the material from without, rather than soaking through from the inside. Likewise, there was no telltale pool of blood adjacent to his torso to suggest that there was any hemorrhage on the side of his body that was pressed to the floor.

"Jarvis?" Pryce said after a beat.

"It's true," I replied. "There are no signs of trauma about his person aside what looks like the early stages of a black eye."

"Could there be some sort of internal damage?" Pryce asked.

I cocked my head, considering. "Possibly, but I'm not sure how it could have been inflicted without any outward —" I paused, an idea springing to mind. "This may be a laughable suggestion, but would it be possible to achieve something of that nature with glamour?"

"No glamour," Miss Sherwood and Goodfellow said in unison, and I was reminded that they would be able to see manifestations of Folk power that would be invisible to the human eye.

"Interesting," Lester mused. "That would suggest the perpetrator was human. But writing 'sais' on the wall indicates exactly the opposite."

Still on hands and knees, Miss Sherwood made her way over to the body, settling next to it opposite me. "Shall we see what else the victim may yet be able to tell us?"

At first, I did not take her meaning, but then she made a small pushing gesture, and I realized she wanted to roll the body over. After a moment's hesitation, I nodded and was reaching out to complete the task when, to my great surprise, she did the same. I have seen grown men, soldiers even, quail at the prospect of handling a corpse, but she didn't so much as blink. Together, we eased the poor man onto his back, whereupon I moved his arm out of the way.

Once he was arranged to Miss Sherwood's satisfaction, she took up a length of silk from her bag and spread it out on the floor, careful not to disturb any of the gory debris. Then she began—somewhat ruthlessly, in my opinion— rifling through the man's pockets and withdrawing whatever objects she found, describing each as she deposited it upon the silk.

"Gold watch by" —she squinted at the maker's mark— "Barraud, of London. Gold chain, very heavy and solid. Leather case containing cards printed with the name Enoch J. Drebber. Handkerchief embroidered with the same initials—stitching looks professional, so likely a purchase rather than a sentimental gift. Purse containing... seven pounds thirteen. Two letters—one addressed to Lieutenant E. J. Drebber and one to a Mr. Joseph Stangerson." She paused to look up at us. "Do those names sound familiar?" Both Pryce and the constables shook their heads. Miss Sherwood sat back on her heels and scrutinized the inventory. Then, after a long moment, she reached out to peel back the man's eyelids one by one, and—I can still hardly believe it—leaned forward to *sniff his lips*. With a speculative expression but no explanation, she returned to an upright position and turned her eyes to Lester.

"You can take him away now," she said with an air of abstraction. "I don't think there's much more we can learn."

The chief nodded and motioned to the constables standing near the door, who ducked out and returned shortly with a stretcher. I made to regain my feet and move out of their way when a glint caught my eye near the victim's hip, partially obscured by the tail of his coat.

"What's this?" I said aloud, reaching for it.

"What's what?" Miss Sherwood echoed.

Lifting the object into the light, I could perceive that it was a ring—specifically a band of blossoms fashioned from rose gold, each bearing a tiny piece of onyx or some other dark gemstone in its center. The delicate beauty of the piece was so antithetical to the setting that it took me a moment to fully take in what I was seeing, but even once I had, it was hard to make heads or tails of its presence. Why would the victim have had such a thing?

"May I?" Miss Sherwood said, and when I looked up, I could see that the air of rumination she had taken on was gone and that her gaze was once again sharp and assessing. I handed her the ring, and she turned it over in her fingers, cocking her head.

"It's Folk craft for sure," she said. "Poppies…odd." She met my gaze. "Bands of flowers like this are popular amongst wights and elementals, often gifted by sweethearts. But the blooms are usually something more romantic, such as roses or gardenias. Poppies must have held a special meaning for the woman this piece belonged to."

Lester raised his eyebrows. "Are you suggesting that the murderer was female?

"Not at all," Miss Sherwood said, rising to her feet. I hurried to follow suit, finally making way for the stretcher. "The murderer was a man, in excess of six feet tall. He wore square-toed boots that would be considered average on a human male, but large for one of the Folk, dependent on his pedigree; one boot was nicked in the heel. The suspect would likely be identifiable by a florid face and notably long fingernails." She approached Robin Goodfellow, heedless of the looks of stupefaction on the rest of our faces. "The ring must have had significant sentimental value to him, though, to keep it close enough to his person that he carried it with him to the scene of a crime." She handed the token to Goodfellow who examined it wordlessly before tucking it into his waistcoat pocket.

"Then you believe the ring belonged to the murderer and not the victim?" Pryce asked.

"I do," she said. "Though it would help to know…" Her gaze snapped to Lester. "Is the constable who discovered the body still present?"

"He should be," the chief replied. "Fellow named John Rance—he was outside last I saw him."

Miss Sherwood nodded and, taking up one of the lanterns, made her way to the door. Goodfellow followed her without hesitation, and after exchanging a wary look, Lester, Pryce, and I trailed along behind them like ducklings.

In the yard, she walked up to the cluster of officers still huddled against the wall. "Excuse me, is one of you John Rance?"

"That's me, miss," one of them said, slipping into automatic deference at the sound of a feminine voice, but looking somewhat taken aback by Miss Sherwood's attire and general demeanor.

"Would you mind answering a few questions for me, Constable Rance? About the murder?"

His brow furrowed in consternation, but he only said, "Yes, miss."

"How did you come upon the body?"

"Well," he began. "I was just doing my rounds, you see —we've increased patrols around this area since construction began—when I saw another constable come tearing out of this cottage, blowing his whistle to wake the dead. I hurried over to see what had him riled, and he told me there was a body in here, barely cold. Well, I went over a bit light-headed for a moment—we don't actually see much in the way of trouble on a typical night, and certainly nothing like murder." I glanced at Pryce, remembering what he'd said about the force's utility, or lack thereof. "I made to go back to the lane, rouse a stableboy or somesuch to head to the station and summon backup, but the first constable, he said he'd go for help, that I should just stay here and keep an eye on things until he came back. So that's what I did. I went in and had a proper look around, but I didn't want to touch anything until the others arrived. I kept thinking they'd be here any minute, but it felt like an age that I was waiting. Finally, though, I saw Lester there coming down the lane with some of the other boys, and we've all been here ever since."

"Tell me about your boots, Constable Rance," Miss Sherwood said, bending over to cast the light from her lantern over the constable's feet.

"My... boots?" he said, looking down. The footwear in question was fairly unremarkable, rounded at the toe and slightly worn at the heels, but well cared for. I wasn't sure quite what Miss Sherwood was getting at.

"Yes. Where did you get them? Are they issued to you with the uniform?"

"No, miss. It's only the clothes and the helmet that are given to us—we're expected to wear our own boots."

"Does everybody in your ranks wear boots like yours? Or is there someone who favors something heavier, with a square toe?"

"I... don't recall seeing anything of that description," he said slowly, looking to us in a plea for elucidation, which we were hard-pressed to offer.

Miss Sherwood's gaze was unwavering. "Constable Rance," she said. "Did you recognize the man blowing the whistle?"

Rance shifted uncomfortably. "Well, it was dark, you see. And his face was in shadow there in the lane, I couldn't make out much besides the coat and helmet—"

"Come now," Miss Sherwood said, her tone insistent but not unkind. "There can't be many of you on the force.

Surely, you'd get to know each other's miens and mannerisms. Did you recognize him?"

Rance's eyes fell to his boots once more. "No," he said, very quietly.

"And did he return with Lester and the others?

"No," he said again, still barely above a whisper. "I did wonder about that, but when I asked, Thompson there said it was a boy that came to get them. Told him that a constable had given him a tuppence to deliver the message that they were needed. And then we all got busy, and I didn't think about it again."

Miss Sherwood let out a plaintive breath.

"That was your murderer, constable. And he walked away, free as air."

Rance stared at her for a moment, but then it seemed that hearing the allegation stated so baldly rather than just implied galvanized him a bit.

"But that makes no sense! He was the one who sounded the alarm. He was the one who drew my attention to the cottage by blowing his whistle. Why would he have done that if he was the murderer? He'd have been caught quicker than you can say Jack Robinson!"

"And did you catch him?" she said.

Rance gaped at her for a long moment, then snapped his mouth shut. His eyes went glassy as his attention retreated inward; one could practically see the cogs in his mind turning as he tried to determine what exactly had happened in the previous sixty seconds. Miss Sherwood, seeming to recognize his turmoil, raised a tentative hand and settled it on his arm.

"Thank you for your assistance, Constable Rance. Perhaps this would be a good time for you to consider new professional opportunities, hmm?"

Rance went on staring at her in bewilderment until one

of the other constables took him by the elbow, murmuring something into his ear. The two of them moved on then, followed by the others of their brethren who had been milling around, but not before Rance's escort shot Miss Sherwood a venomous look over his shoulder. Once the five of us were alone, Goodfellow sighed.

"Well, there's a man who will spend the rest of the evening reevaluating the entire course of his life. At least until he passes out from drink."

"Nothing I said was personal," Miss Sherwood said, a touch defensively. "I only presented the facts."

Goodfellow's face softened a bit.

"I know, my dear. But we've been over this. Sometimes people are not ready to hear such unvarnished truths."

Miss Sherwood crossed her arms over her chest, her face pensive.

"In any case," Pryce intervened. "What are we to do now?"

"The queen will not be pleased," Goodfellow said. "We all know her patience with Cavendish is nearing a breaking point. This could give her the excuse to break diplomatic ties altogether."

"But the victim is not formally attached to the embassy —surely, she wouldn't…" I trailed off at the grave look on Goodfellow's face. If I had given a thought to my words before speaking, I might have realized that everyone present understood the nuances of relations here on the island better than I did.

"The graffiti does suggest Folk involvement," Pryce said. "That would take the pressure off of Cavendish."

"On the contrary," Goodfellow said. "It would imply that the British presence here is causing increased unrest. It's no secret that many attached to the delegation harbor anti-Folk sentiments." I swallowed, and Pryce looked abashed, but we could hardly deny it. "Together with the isolationist rhetoric she hears day in and day out, this could be enough for her to draw us back into seclusion, cut off from the human world entirely."

"Well, then," said Miss Sherwood. "We just need to find the murderer. If we figure out what happened, it will go a long way towards assuaging fears and maintaining the peace."

Her voice was confident, and there was a determined set to her jaw, but in that moment, I felt a pang on her behalf. I had only just met Miss Sherwood; I knew nothing of her past or her current situation, beyond a few broad strokes. Still, I wondered what it must be like for her, hearing the prospect of estrangement between humans and Folk discussed as a matter of significance, but only on the grand scale of politics. If Mab decided to sever relations, it would be a blow to all of us, but we at the embassy had our everyday, conventional lives to go back to; the injury would not be grievous. Such was not the case for Miss Sherwood. With her background, the situation was deeply personal.

After a long moment, Goodfellow spoke again.

"This is a delicate matter, gentlemen. May we depend upon your cooperation?"

I was struck by the oddness of the request. Nevermind the rather pedantic question of where each of us fell within the political hierarchy on the island—we were being asked by one of the most legendary Folk in the British Isles to assist in a murder investigation with the daughter of one of the most notorious noblemen in the British Empire. In my wildest imaginings, I couldn't have predicted it, and the task almost certainly fell outside the scope of our duties. But truly, what else could we say but…

"Yes," Pryce replied. "Of course."

Goodfellow gave a nod of acknowledgment. "Miss Sherwood and I will call on you at your offices in the morning, if that suits."

Pryce gave a slight bow. "I will inform the colonel." And after that, there was very little left to say. With murmured farewells, Goodfellow and Miss Sherwood withdrew to make their way back to the high street, where a carriage awaited them. Pryce thanked Lester once more, and we took our leave.

Our return trip to the center of the Quarter felt shorter than the walk out, but also more somber; Pryce and I spoke very little, caught up in our own speculations. As we approached our cottages, a figure came stumbling into view from the other direction. When we were close enough to identify in the moonlight, I saw that it was Waddington. He seemed quite the worse for drink; his unbuttoned jacket flapped open with every motion, and his hair was disheveled, which I could tell because his hat was nowhere in evidence. When he caught sight of us, he came to a precarious stop at the edge of the path and gave us a genial, if graceless, wave.

"Ho!" he called. "Where have you chaps been off to? Is it anything to do with the murder?"

Well, now we knew that the secret was out.

"It was," Pryce said, in a tone clearly meant to discourage further conversation. "Tomorrow, we'll start working through the standard procedure—"

"Was it something very gruesome?" Waddington continued, swaying on his feet. "A crime of passion?"

Pryce sighed. "I don't see how that's—"

"I heard it was an army man. Anyone we know?"

"No," Pryce said, obviously nearing the end of his patience. "It wasn't anybody attached to the island. Fellow named Drebber."

The transformation that came over Waddington was as surprising as it was immediate. His intoxicated bonhomie evaporated, and it was difficult to tell for sure in the low light, but it seemed he went pale.

"Drebber? Is that what you said?"

"Why, yes," Pryce replied, cocking his head at the shift in Waddington's demeanor.

Waddington swayed a bit. "And you're sure?"

"Yes." A note of concern entered Pryce's voice as he took a step forward. "I say, Waddington, are you all right?"

"Yes," Waddington replied quickly, shaking off his stupor. "Fine. That punch at the ball was deuced strong is all." This assertion rang false to me, as I knew he regularly availed himself of libations far more potent than anything that would be considered appropriate for mixed company. I had little opportunity to challenge him on this point, though, as he was had started creeping backwards. "I'm sure a good night's sleep will set me right. Evening, gentleman."

Then he hurried into his cottage and slammed the door. Pryce and I stared after him for a long moment.

"Well, that was… odd," I said finally.

Pryce pinched the bridge of his nose, letting out a long exhale.

"It has been a long day," he said. "I am absolutely knackered and in desperate need of tea. I am now going into my house, where I will spend the rest of the night in peaceful and pleasant solitude, and we will deal with this in the morning. Am I clear?"

"Yes, sir," I murmured, and he stalked up the path to his cottage.

I thought tea actually sounded like a capital idea, so once I had settled in my own abode and changed out of my uniform, I made some and began to write. It is late now, but I wanted to be sure to commit the account of this very strange night to paper while it was fresh in my mind. I hope it does not infiltrate my dreams.

We shall see what transpires tomorrow, I suppose. I cannot imagine it will be the match of today.

Your brother,
Wilf

Chapter 9

scaphoid, lunate, triquetrum, pisiform, trapezium, capitate, hama

21 March 1881

Dear Esther,

I was mistaken. Today was every bit as strange as the last.

I woke later than is typically my habit. One upshot of the embassy community observing London customs is that they also observe London hours. Typically, this makes no difference to me, as I still arrive at the office around 8:30 and work in peaceable silence with Pryce until the colonel and Waddington arrive sometime after 10. After my late night, however, I was relieved to get an extra bit of rest.

Once out of bed, I dressed, shaved, and ate a quick breakfast of toast and tea. I was just getting ready to head to the office when there was a knock on the door. I couldn't think of anyone who would be calling on me at that time of day, so it was with some perplexity that I opened the door.

A woman, wrinkled and hunched with age, stood before me; I had to debate for a moment whether she was a human or a gnome, before settling on the former due to the lack of beard. She was clad neck to foot in garments that were neat but faded, their original quality worn down to something that just passed for respectable, giving her extravagant hat—a straw number resplendent with feathers and cherries—pride of place. Wisps of grey hair peeked out from beneath the hat's brim, and she held a knotted walking stick in her equally gnarled hands.

"Can I help you?" I said.

"Good morning, doctor," the woman replied in Honoria Sherwood's voice and, without waiting for an invitation, swept past me into the house. She removed her hat and placed it on the coat rack, smoothing her silvery curls as she made her way across the small parlor and into my study. After a moment of utter astonishment, I closed the door and followed her.

When I entered, she was making a circuit of the room, examining the furnishings, sparse as they were, with the same attentiveness that she had exhibited at the crime scene the night before, an exercise which did little to settle my nerves. She paused to examine the handful of books I had actually unloaded from crates and place onto shelves, the fossilized ammonite I brought back from the shore at Lyme Regis, my boxing trophy from university. At this, she raised her eyebrows and turned to me.

"You are a pugilist?"

"Not anymore—I was back at school. And sorry, but what exactly is it you're doing here? I thought you were planning to consult with us at the embassy."

"Well, yes," she said as she wandered over to the

window and peeked out. "We were going to do that. But upon reflection, I decided we might have better luck with an alternate course of action. So I put it out amongst the servants that a ring had been lost and might be claimed after luncheon."

"And you said they were supposed to come *here*?"

"It seemed wise," she said, her voice even. "Your office would have aroused far too much suspicion. This comes across as more neutral ground."

"You can literally see the office from that window, so I'm not sure how this ground is more neutral," I said. "Plus, I'm needed at the office! I have work to do!"

"Oh, no need to worry about that," she said. "Robin is taking care of it."

"Miss Sherwood," I said, struggling to keep my emotions under control. "This kind of interference is most irregular and, if I may be frank, unwelcome. I serve at Her Majesty Queen Victoria's pleasure, not yours. To say nothing of the fact that you are here without a chaperone!"

"Yes, that *is* the primary reason I took the precaution of wearing a disguise." She picked up the small framed photograph of Ella that sat on my desk, studying it. "She's lovely. Daughter?"

"Niece. I am not married. There is also the small detail that we don't actually have the ring in question."

Without a word, she replaced the photo, reached into the purse at her belt, and produced a small metallic object that she held out for my inspection. Taking it, I discovered it was a band of poppies, quite similar to the one we had found at the crime scene.

"It was short notice, but I managed to find a reasonable facsimile," she said. "That one wouldn't fool an individual who cherished the other, but it should serve well

75

enough to convince someone who had seen it in passing, which I suspect is all we require of it."

"And how, pray tell, am I supposed to explain your presence here?"

"I don't know. Say I'm the housekeeper."

"I don't have a housekeeper!"

"Yes," she said, running a finger along the edge of a shelf, then inspecting it with a grimace before brushing it off on her skirt. "I had deduced as much. All the more reason for you to engage my services."

"Now, see here—" I began, but just then, there was a knock at the door. We both froze, gazes locked. After a moment, Miss Sherwood made a visible effort to collect herself.

"Go sit at the desk," she said brusquely. "Make yourself look busy. I'll see whoever it is in."

With that, she turned and hurried to the foyer. For lack of any real alternatives, I did as she said. Taking stock of what was available to me to lend credence to this charade, I realized I had little to work with—only a pen, inkstand and blotter, the photograph of Ella, and this diary. I heard voices approaching, and, in a panic, I snatched up the diary and began writing the first thing that came into my head, which was the names of the bones in the hand. There was a soft knock at the study door, and Miss Sherwood, hunched over and moving with a shuffling gait, stepped into the room followed by a much younger woman.

"A Miss Linetta to see you, sir," said Miss Sherwood in an uncanny imitation of a crone's grating rasp. Closing my diary, I stood to greet this Linetta. I could tell by her delicate prettiness that she was one of the elemental Folk known as sylphs, whose particular affinity is air. Indeed, with her fine-boned frame, wide blue eyes, and cloud of blonde hair, one half expected her to drift from place to place rather than walk. But while Folk of her kind often exhibited a dreamlike demeanor, her own face showed evidence of strain and worry.

"My lord," she said with a curtsy that left me rather flustered.

"Oh, no," I hurried to correct her. I'm not entirely sure how such a misconception could have arisen. Perhaps to the common Folk, everyone at the embassy is of noble blood? "I am merely a surgeon—you may refer to me as 'doctor'. Dr. Wilfred Jarvis."

"Oh," she said. "All right. Thank you… doctor."

"Won't you sit?" I asked, extending my hand to the chair facing my desk, and Linetta accepted my invitation, perching on the seat and casting a curious look around the room. Miss Sherwood reached into the nearest open crate and began pulling out books. Having produced a feather duster, from where I cannot even begin to guess, she gave each book a quick going-over, and placed it on the shelf. Evidently, she had no intention of absenting herself from the conversation that was about to commence.

Once again seated, I settled my linked hands on the desk blotter in front of me. "What can I do for you, Miss Linetta?"

She still looked unsure of herself, but she held herself straight as she said, "It's only that I heard from Isa at the market that someone found a ring yesterday evening, and that we might call here to see after it. Is that right, my —doctor?"

"It is," I said, reaching into my pocket to retrieve the ring that Miss Sherwood had given me. I placed it on the blotter and slid it toward her. "Do you recognize this?"

At the sight of the ring, Linetta's face lit up. "Oh," she breathed as she reached forward and picked up the ring, turning it in her fingers so that it caught the light streaming in through the study windows. Tears welled in her eyes, and without a word, I offered her my handkerchief. As she dabbed at her eyes, I considered her, wondering how to proceed. Her emotion seemed genuine, but I couldn't fathom how she could be connected to the scene from the previous night. Over her shoulder, I caught sight of Miss Sherwood, who made a not-terribly subtle get-on-with-it gesture. I cleared my throat.

"It must be an enormous relief to have it back in your possession," I said, feeling ungainly and awkward, but she did not seem to notice.

"Oh, it's not mine," she said distractedly, blotting her nose delicately. "Rather, it is my sister's ring."

"Your sister's?" I repeated, and she froze, a flicker of horror passing over her face. She had let something slip, something she hadn't wanted us to know. I felt an odd surge of triumph but knew better than to show it.

"Well, I'm sure she will be delighted to have it back," I said blandly, brushing an imaginary speck of dust from the desktop, and she relaxed a bit. That was good. If she didn't think I'd noticed her slip, she might yet give us more information to go on.

Miss Sherwood drifted towards us with her feather duster and glanced casually over Linetta's shoulder.

"Oh, my, that is lovely," she said, eyes wide. "I'd be in a tizzy if I had something like that go missing. Where did she lose it?"

Miss Sherwood's wrinkled face was all innocent curiosity, but I could still see uncertainty in Linetta's eyes. After a moment, she gave Miss Sherwood a valiant but not terribly convincing smile.

"She wasn't sure what happened," she said, and I could tell she was selecting her words with care. "She does odd jobs all over the island, you see, and when she got home, she couldn't remember when she'd last seen the ring on her finger." She turned her attention to me. "Where did you find it?"

In my peripheral vision, I saw Miss Sherwood's nostril's flare, but she did not otherwise react. I was impressed, because I myself was having a difficult time maintaining my composure. I suspected Linetta was a dab hand at poker, because she had taken the cards we'd dealt her and played them exceedingly well. Now, we were the ones on the defensive. I did my best to keep my voice breezy as I responded.

"Oh, it had fallen in between some cobbles down near the shops," I said, and then, for good measure, "I saw it as I was coming out of the apothecary."

Linetta nodded. "Ah, yes, that makes sense. She had some errands to run around there. It must have fallen off without her noticing."

I couldn't quite read the look on her face, but whatever her state of mind, she had apparently decided there was no benefit in prolonging her visit any further. She slipped the ring into her reticule, then folded my handkerchief into a neat square and passed it back to me. I found the whole scenario most perplexing. She was obviously lying about the conditions under which the ring had gone missing, but her relief upon seeing it had been sincere. Was this sister of hers real, or some kind of ruse? It had seemed the former in the moment, but why had she gone so cagey all of a sudden? She had obviously been trying to get information from us, just as we were from her, but to what end? What did all of it mean?

Miss Sherwood went back to her dusting as we got to our feet, and I came around the desk to escort Linetta out. When the door closed behind her, I turned and nearly leaped out of my skin to find Miss Sherwood directly at my back.

"Well, what are you waiting for?" she snapped. "Go after her!"

I gaped at her. "Me?"

"Yes, you! I am supposed to be an old woman! I won't be able to move with anything approaching speed or stealth in this getup."

"And you think I'll go unnoticed, following a lone young woman of the Folk whilst in full uniform?"

Her eyes narrowed. "While you stand here quibbling, she is getting further away, and we are losing our potential chance to learn something about the murder."

I opened my mouth to show her some real quibbling, but then decided that, however infuriatingly, she was right. With a sigh, I grabbed my hat and made my way out the front door, onto the high street.

It was a fine day, and the sun was pleasant on my shoulders. I was careful to maintain a suitable distance from Linetta, irrationally but entirely convinced that someone would leap from an obscure alleyway to grab me by the scruff of the neck and loudly pronounce me a predatory deviant of the worst type. It perhaps goes without saying that this did not happen. As I walked, I came across several residents of the Quarter that I was coming to recognize from my daily peregrinations; they only waved and called out pleasantries, seemingly devoid of suspicion or misgivings. For her part, Miss Linetta progressed resolutely and straight-backed, as if she hadn't a care in the world.

As we neared the dock, I began to wonder if anything was going to happen that would distinguish this bit of espionage from a relaxing constitutional. But then I paused to check for approaching carts on a cross street, and when I looked up at the path again, Linetta was gone.

I froze in my tracks, blinking. The stretch of road she'd just occupied was bordered by a stone wall on one side and the sea, high with the incoming tide, on the other. There were no alleys to duck into, no places to hide. She had literally disappeared right in front of me. Vanished into thin air.

Because of course—she was a sylph. Air was her element.

After staring balefully at the empty prospect before me for a bit longer, I turned and began trudging my way home.

Miss Sherwood pounced on me as soon as I entered the house.

"Well? Where did she go?"

"I'm not sure. I followed her until we neared the dock, and then she disappeared."

Miss Sherwood was incredulous. "You lost her?!"

"I did not *lose* her," I said, striving to maintain my calm. "She winked out of existence directly in front of me."

She'd already opened her mouth to further berate me, but at this she paused, then seemed to deflate.

"I forget sometimes," she said. "That none of you can see through the facade of glamour." She sank into one of the desk chairs, leaning against the back in a most desultory fashion.

I hadn't noticed, until that moment, how insistently she referred to myself and other humans as "you", when her own father was one of us. It hardly seemed the time for such an observation, however, so I merely claimed a chair of my own.

"It seemed like a good plan," she said, frustration clear

in her tone. "But I left a key factor out of my calculations and now look. Nothing to show for it."

"Not nothing," I said, not entirely sure why I felt the need to bolster her confidence. "You have a new lead. You can look into this Linetta—"

"If that even is her real name," Miss Sherwood grumbled.

"And find out what connection she could have to this" —here I cast my mind back to her description from the night before— "tall human chap with heavy boots and a ruddy face."

"He'd also likely have a persistent sniffle," she said distractedly. "Or at the very least a hyponasal manner of speaking."

I stared at her.

"How do you do that?"

Her brow furrowed as she shifted her eyes to me. "Do what?"

"Summon up knowledge about everything from chamber music to footwear. Make connections that no one else can see."

Her cheeks colored. "Well, I read. I study."

"I read and study," I said. "I went to medical school, for pity's sake. I can't do what you do."

Her face was unreadable, but I had the impression I was being weighed and measured.

"Well, I like solving puzzles," she said. "The more things I know, the more puzzles I can solve. So I do my best to know a lot of things."

"But your deductions, the lighting quick calculations you make, just... how?"

"I don't know," she said, and there was no hint of boasting in her tone as she gazed at me with those clear grey eyes. "I just do. I always have."

I tried to imagine her as a child, terrorizing nursemaids and uncovering the schemes of overmatched playmates. What a fearsome thing she must have been.

"Explain it to me," I said.

She raised her eyebrows. "What?"

"Your process. For example, how were you able to determine his height? What leaps did you take to come to your conclusion?"

She was quiet for a moment, but I could see that active mind working away behind her eyes. Was she usually so reticent to discuss her methods of deduction? Or had nobody ever asked her about them before?

"It was the length of the stride," she said finally, and I recalled her crawling around on the floor, measuring something I couldn't identify at the time. "Plus the writing on the wall. Typically, someone undertaking such an endeavor would do so at roughly the level of their own eyes." She held up a finger and demonstrated in the air in front of her. "Taken together, those pieces of evidence are practically ironclad."

"What about the fingernails?"

"That was also the wall. The writing had obviously been done with a finger dipped in blood. When I examined it with my magnifying glass, I could see that the plaster was scratched in concert with the shape of the letters, which would not have been the case if the man's nails had been trimmed."

"And the sniffle?"

"That's on account of the snuff—Lundyfoot, if I am not mistaken, based on its light color and fine texture."

I blinked. "Is our man a visitor from the time of George III? Snuff was considered passé in my grandfather's time."

"I make no speculation as to the suspect's origins," she

said, seemingly in complete earnest. "I am only reporting what I see."

"And what of your attire?" I said. "Have you trained for the stage?"

"After a fashion," she said, then laughed at my surprised reaction. "My sister Constancia and I used to put on amateur theatricals when we were younger. I picked up a few tricks. But do you remember what you said last night, that you knew music, but it was your sister who was the real musician in the family?" she said, and I nodded. "It is the same with Constancia and me. I have some aptitude for the dramatic arts, but she is the true thespian."

"I think I should like to meet her," I said. "Does she live here on the island as well?"

"She does, usually, but at present, she is staying with our grandmother in Yorkshire." Her face went a little wistful. "I miss her dreadfully."

"Are the two of you very much alike?"

Miss Sherwood laughed again. "Oh, not at all. And we often fight like cats when she is here. But the house is too quiet without her." Her smile faded, her focus turning inward. "Growing up, it was only the pair of us. The... unique makeup of our family made socializing difficult. It was challenging to build friendships with either the Folk or the humans of our acquaintance. As a result, we are quite devoted to each other."

She said this matter-of-factly, but I felt a pang in my chest, an echo of the loneliness she must have experienced, with only one other equally isolated child for company. I gazed at her impassive face, touched by the afternoon sunlight, and wondered what was truly going on inside her head.

Noticing the sunlight made me realize how much time had passed. I knew that it was time for her to go—that I really should have sent her home the moment she appeared on my doorstep—but I found that, for all that she was an overbearing, unchaperoned daughter of a baronet, I didn't especially want her to leave.

"So, what now?" I said. "Are you going to check into Linetta?"

She huffed out an irritated breath. "I would like nothing better, but I cannot. I am expected at holiday observances this afternoon and then the ball at the castle this evening."

"What, another one?"

"Oh, last night's didn't count," she said. "We both know it was just elaborate posturing. This one is far more in keeping with the spirit of the day." She stood, prompting me to do the same. "Before I go, is there anything you can think of that may come into play here. Did you notice anything before you lost Linetta?"

I debated correcting her again, but her tone had lost its accusatory note, so I let the slip pass. "No. Nothing springs to mind." I paused, remembering. "Although there was one thing…"

Her eyes lit with interest.

"Oh? And what was that?"

"Pryce and I ran into our colleague Waddington last night after we left the crime scene…" I stumbled a bit at that, my words sounding like a penny dreadful to my own ears. "He was just coming back from the assembly rooms, and when Pryce told him the dead man's name, he looked as if he'd seen a ghost. But when we tried to ask him about it, he scurried inside and slammed the door."

"Waddington," she said thoughtfully. "Isn't he the pretty one with the curls?"

I wasn't entirely sure about the pretty part, but the curls were accurate enough, so I nodded.

"Hmmm," she continued. "Interesting."

"How so?"

"He keeps peculiar company. I've heard mention of him spending time with both humans on the island who aren't fond of Folk and Folk who aren't fond of humans."

"Fingers in all the wrong pies," I said, and she nodded.

"It makes one wonder," she said. I considered this for a moment.

"Hardly seems the type to commit murder, though."

She raised her eyebrows. "Is this soldierly allegiance coming to the fore? You defend him because he is your brother at arms?"

"Not at all," I said, failing to suppress a snort. "It's only that committing a murder seems more... taxing? Than he would like?"

The corner of her mouth quirked up. "Do you mean he's lazy?"

"Not lazy, exactly," I said. "More... indolent?"

"So, lazy."

I chuckled. "Yes, alright, I suppose so."

She gave me a full smile then, but it was wary. "Never rely on your suppositions, doctor. In instances such as these, only evidence will guide you to the truth."

We stood there facing each other for a moment, the silence between us feeling slightly charged. Something about that energy felt precarious, like standing on the edge of a cliff; I felt a sudden urge to dispel it and motioned to the entry.

"I do hope you enjoy your evening," I said. She gave me a knowing look, as if she understood some of what I was doing, but she said nothing as she retrieved her hat.

"Please keep us apprised of whatever you discover next," I said opening the front door for her.

"Oh, I will," she replied and stepped over the threshold, the cherries on her chapeau bobbing merrily. "Who knows? I may even be able to put my time at the ball to use. You'd be shocked what people are comfortable sharing on a crowded dance floor."

I shook my head. "Good afternoon, Miss Sherwood."

"Good afternoon, Dr. Jarvis," she replied, with an inclination of her head. Then she turned, and I watched her until she reached the end of the path.

I had intended to go to the office once she'd left, but standing there in the quiet, I decided I didn't want to. Goodfellow had made my excuses, after all, and if I was truly needed, Pryce would probably send Waddington around to collect me. Perhaps it would be all right to take a bit of a day to myself.

So I went to my study and began unpacking books.

Your brother,

Wilf

Chapter 10

22 March 1881

DEAR ESTHER,

Upon my arrival at the office this morning, Pryce was most curious as to what had kept me away the day before. He cornered me in the reception area as soon as I arrived.

"Goodfellow came himself to discuss the matter with the colonel," he said, a touch of awe in his voice. "I've never seen a wight do something like that before. What exactly did you and Miss Sherwood get up to?"

The wording of the question got my hackles up a bit, with its seeming implication of something untoward, but I knew Pryce well enough by now to understand he was not prone to puerile speculation; he was genuinely interested in the case. As I recounted the events of the day before, he pursed his lips, looking thoughtful.

"A sylph, eh? That's interesting."

"How so?"

"Sylphs aren't exactly known for having strong

passions. They are typically gentle creatures. I wouldn't expect one to be tangled up in something like this."

"Well, clearly, we're looking at her as an accomplice and not the actual murderer," I said. "Plus, her involvement would be consistent with the evidence at the scene. The writing on the wall did signify the involvement of the Folk." As I came to the end of these observations, it occurred to me both that Miss Sherwood would likely appreciate my logic and that I was pleased about it.

"You're right," Pryce conceded, tapping his chin. "But even so…" He grew thoughtful for a moment, then shook his head. "I suppose we'll see what Miss Sherwood uncovers next. In the meantime, I have work to do." And his disappeared down the hallway to his office.

The reality was that I, too, had work that needed attention, especially after being out the day before. I went to my office as well, but I didn't stay long. There were documents that needed to be typed up, and while our workspace boasted polished woods, beautiful stained glass windows, and intricate crown molding, it only contained a single working typewriter that was kept out front for all of us to use. I had been working away on it for an hour or so when I heard the door open and looked up to find Miss Sherwood standing on the other side of the railing.

"Miss Sherwood," I said, somewhat taken aback. It hit me in a flash that this was the first time I'd seen her in everyday clothing rather than a formal gown, costume, or borrowed menswear. Her dress was blue, but of a deeper shade and simpler cut than her ball gown, and her hair was gathered at the base of her neck in a simple knot. She again wore a snake necklace, but this one was only a simple gold pendant on a delicate chain. Altogether, she looked quite fetching.

And also, furious.

I realized I was staring and leapt to my feet, face warm. "What brings you here today?"

"Was it you?" she said with some heat and, if I wasn't mistaken, a note of betrayal.

I blinked. "Was what me?"

"One of the townsfolk in Glastonbury has been arrested for Drebber's murder. Did you have anything to do with it?"

"No," I said, startled by the accusation, and more wounded than I would have anticipated. "I haven't spoken to anyone about the murder since we parted ways yesterday."

"Well, to the best of my knowledge, you and I are the only ones who have been pursuing this matter in earnest, and I haven't taken any action that would result in such an outcome," she said, eyes flashing. "So, unless the human authorities have started detaining citizens at random, I'm not sure who else it could have been!"

"Is there something we can help you with, Miss Sherwood?" a voice said, and turning, I saw Pryce standing in the doorway that led back to the private offices. Waddington hovered behind him, munching on an apple. Apparently, Miss Sherwood's protestations had carried sufficiently to arouse attention. If she was at all cowed by this state of affairs, though, she didn't show it.

"I was merely trying to ascertain if Dr. Jarvis was involved in the apprehension of an *innocent man*"—here, she gave me a hard look, despite my assertion of own innocence—"for the murder of Enoch Drebber in town yesterday evening."

"Oh, no" Waddington said around a mouthful of apple, surprising everyone. He swallowed. "That was my doing."

We all stared at him.

"Yours?" I said, plainly doing a poor job of hiding my surprise, because he gave me a petulant sniff.

"Why so shocked? You don't think me capable of taking initiative on behalf of justice?"

"Waddington," Pryce said. "In our lengthy acquaintance, I have never known you to take initiative on behalf of anything besides your own gross self-interest. I see no reason for you to start now."

Waddington scowled and turned away. I thought for a moment he was going to storm off in a huff, but he merely tossed his apple core into a wastebasket before facing us again and crossing his arms over his chest.

"Colonel Abercrombie *may* have intimated that I wasn't entirely pulling my weight around here, and it seemed like this could be an opportunity to get into his good graces. There, happy?"

Pryce and I exchanged a look. Our encounter with Waddington on the night of the murder suggested that a more personal connection was in play, but he clearly didn't want to discuss it; if we forced the issue, we could lose a chance to gain some valuable insight. Pryce sighed.

"Please continue."

Waddington gave a smug nod of assent. "We had the poor sod's name, and he couldn't have been staying on the island, so I went into town and started checking around at boarding houses. Took a few tries, but I eventually ended up at one called Charpentier's. Decent place—not fancy or anything, but respectable. The proprietress was a handsome middle-aged woman who invited me into the parlor for tea. There was a younger woman there already, quite a looker, who I later learned was the landlady's daughter. Anyway, once the tea things were settled, I asked if the establishment had lately had a boarder by the name of Enoch Drebber. At the mention of the name, the daughter gasped and dropped her needlework. That obviously seemed fishy, but when I started to ask her about it, the mother interceded. She made a great show of asking about the nature of my interest in the man, clearly trying to distract me, but it ended up not doing any good in the long run, because as soon as I explained that I was investigating Drebber's murder, the girl erupted into hysterical tears.

"Well, after a lot of waffling, I finally got it out of them that Drebber *had* been a guest at their establishment, staying there with his secretary, a fellow named Stangerson, and, evidently, he had gotten handsy with the young Miss Charpentier on numerous occasions."

Pryce's eyebrows shot up, while Miss Sherwood's mouth tightened into an expression that communicated revulsion, but not surprise.

"She didn't report this behavior to anyone?" Pryce said. Waddington shrugged.

"She did not. She said she didn't want to deprive her mother of a paying customer. At any rate, around this time her brother came home on leave from the merchant marine, and he stumbled across the two of them as Drebber was making one of his advances. The way the girl told it, the brother pulled Drebber off of her and set about trying to thrash the life out of him. Somehow, Drebber was able to get away, but the brother gave chase. The girl said she figured the boy would return once he was satisfied he'd put the fear of God into Drebber, but that didn't happen. She said she waited and waited, but he didn't return.

"I asked what time he did finally make it back to the boarding house, and both of the women got very quiet. The girl glanced at her mother, who had gone quite white-faced, then back at me. Then she whispered, 'He never came home. We still haven't seen him.'

"The mother was in a right state then, wailing 'How

could you?' and 'You have killed him!', which only made the girl cry harder. I said, 'Ma'am, do you think your son is guilty of a crime that would merit such a consequence?' She swore she did not, but said it clearly seemed to me that he did, which is what would ultimately seal his fate."

"What about this secretary, Stangerson?" said Pryce. "Could he shed any light on the proceedings?"

Waddington shook his head. "He was out in town at the time of the incident. Mrs. Charpentier said he'd been most anxious about his employer when he'd discovered what happened, plaguing her with questions about whether she'd had any news of Drebber. I asked to talk to him myself, but as luck would have it, he had gone out again on some business or other before I'd arrived. Once we'd gotten all of this established, I did my best to set the women's mind at ease. I gave my handkerchief to the girl and explained that I was only after the truth—that if Master Charpentier had not done Drebber any injury, he had nothing to fear.

"The girl just went on sniffling at me, but the mother was able to compose herself. I elicited a promise from them to contact me right away once the man in question resurfaced or Stangerson returned, and Mrs. Charpentier walked me to the door. As she bid me farewell, I could see her mind working, figuring that once I was gone, the family could plot an escape and get the lad beyond our reach before we'd realized what had happened—which was precisely what I had been hoping for. I thought if they felt the worst of the danger had passed, they'd let their guard down. For my part, I left the boarding house and went right to the magistrate.

"After I explained the situation, he sent two of his men with me to watch the boarding house for Mr. Charpentier's return. It took a few hours, but eventually, he did go to ground. Once we saw him go inside, we descended and placed him under arrest. It was quite the scene. One of the magistrate's men placed him in shackles, and we brought him outside into the street as the other ran to fetch the wagon to take him to the local lockup. The women were much as they had been before, the girl standing there on the steps sobbing and the mother caterwauling again about how this would be the death of her son as the neighbors came out to gawk, while the man himself kept protesting that he'd done nothing wrong, only attempted to defend his sister's honor. When we pressed him about his where-abouts at the time of the murder, though, he clammed up. Eventually, the cart came and took him away. Good riddance, I say. This Drebber may have been a bounder, but he didn't deserve to be murdered."

I thought I detected a light sheen of sweat on Waddington's forehead and tried to catch Pryce's eye, but he was focused on Miss Sherwood, who had been listening to the account with a furrowed brow.

"But that is wrong," she said. "The evidence does not support it. There is nothing to suggest—"

"Suggest what?" Waddington cut in. "The poor sod made advances on the wrong girl, and he paid the price for it. It's that… oh, what's it called?" He gestured at Pryce beseechingly. "That shaving thingy you told me about?"

"Occam's razor," Pryce said flatly.

"That's the one!" Waddington said, snapping his fingers. He gave Miss Sherwood a patronizing smile. "The crime has been solved, miss. A dangerous man is off the streets. So, you see, there's no further need for concern."

Miss Sherwood arched an eyebrow. "Oh, really?

"Really." Waddington nodded magnanimously.

"So you've located this Mr. Stangerson? And confirmed that he has a solid alibi?

Waddington's face fell a bit. "Well, no."

"What theories do you have as to how Mr. Charpentier was able to get through the tunnel without a token of his own? And why he would have chosen to bring Lieutenant Drebber onto the island in the first place?"

"I don't… that is to say…"

"Oh, and you must have reached out to Sir Goodfellow about conducting forensic analysis on the evidence collected from Drebber's body—"

"Miss Sherwood!" Waddington snapped, having reached a breaking point. "We are, in fact, professionals here. As representatives of Her Majesty's Army, it is our job to enforce the law in this community to keep the peace." This was a liberal interpretation of our duty at best, but Waddington wasn't letting a little thing like precision get in his way. "Our responsibilities do not include catering to the whims of a spoiled, meddling female who serves up mental parlor tricks to make herself belle of the ball!"

The air in the room fairly hummed with tension when he finished. It was I who ultimately broke the silence.

"You forget yourself, sir. That is no way to speak to a lady."

Waddington made a scoffing sound and looked to Pryce for support, but the captain only stared at him gravely, giving no quarter. A series of emotions played over Waddington's face—dismay, indignation, bitterness—and his lip curled involuntarily before he managed to pull himself together. Straightening his shoulders he turned back to Miss Sherwood.

"I am sorry," he said, sounding anything but. "Please excuse my rudeness."

Miss Sherwood gazed at him wordlessly, her face blank.

Then, cutting a quick look at me, she turned and walked out the door. I followed her directly.

"Miss Sherwood," I called as I hurried along in her wake. "Miss Sherwood!"

She spun on me.

"You needn't have intervened on my behalf that way." Her voice was controlled, but only just; I could hear emotion threatening to burst forth from underneath. This was not at all the reaction I had expected.

"I did not desire your intercession," she continued, "nor do I thank you for it."

"It was the gentlemanly thing to do," I said. "His conduct was disrespectful and inappropriate."

"I agree. But his insult was to the caliber of my reasoning, not to my sex. Any true defense should have addressed the affront as such."

I took a step back, stung, and she gave me a searching look.

"Do you agree with him?"

"What? No!"

"Have you only been humoring me because it is 'gentlemanly'?"

"Of course not," I said, and something inside of me began slipping from dismayed contrition into indignation. "But these things take time—"

"We do not *have* time," she cut in. "I would have thought you of all people would understand that."

"He was trying," I said, realizing with horror as the words came out of my mouth that I was defending *Waddington*, but I couldn't stop. "At least he was going through proper channels, rather than larking about in fancy dress like a—" I did stop then, but it was too late. She recoiled, something almost like grief in her eyes.

"Like a meddling female," she said slowly. "Isn't that

right?" I wanted desperately to say something, try to remedy the situation, but my shame and regret left me speechless. After a long pause, she shook her head.

"*You* forget yourself, doctor," she said, and once more, she turned and left, presumably to do whatever was required to crack the case entirely on her own.

This time, I did not follow her.

Chapter 12

22 March 1881, cont.

IT WAS SUBDUED in the office after she left. I went back to my typing, Waddington stormed off to brood in his office, and at some point, Pryce left to run an errand. I was just pushing away from the typewriter to stretch when Waddington came out into the reception area. He said nothing at first, just went to the window and peered out, as if to check the weather. But eventually, he couldn't help himself.

"All right," he said, turning to me. "I'll concede that I might have been a bit out of line. But my argument was sound."

I sighed and rubbed my face. "Waddington…"

"I mean it," he said, not taking my despair as discouragement. "The magistrate was convinced by the case I presented. Why should her opinion carry more weight than that?"

"Because she is meticulous in her thinking?" I suggested. "Because she has an acutely analytical mind?"

He looked dubious. "But what training has she had? What—"

He cut off at as the front door opened, and Pryce

stepped into the room looking aggravated. His hand was clenched around what looked to be a rather expensive piece of stationery.

"What is it?" I said.

"We've been summoned," he said, holding up the slip of paper. "Lord Evrain wants to see us at the castle."

"What, all of us?" Waddington said, his voice going unusually shrill.

"No," Pryce said. "Only the doctor and I were mentioned by name."

Waddington exhaled in a rush, clearly relieved. "Well, then, I suppose I shall just stay here and hold down the fort. Good luck, chaps!" And he scurried back to his office.

Pryce glared at his retreating back, then turned to me. "Shall we?"

We made most of the journey to the castle in silence. It wasn't until the gates were in view that Pryce said, "Let me do the talking, all right?", which might have offended me if I had any interest at all in speaking for us, but I did not, so I only nodded.

We were ushered through the gate without incident, but rather than taking our usual route to the public rooms, we were led to a wing of the castle primarily devoted to private chambers. Our escort led us to a suite of rooms on the second floor, then bowed in farewell. Our knock was answered by a wight whose attire was simple but clearly expensive. After introducing himself as Lord Evrain's valet, he ushered us into a sitting room that, like the valet's clothing, was both understated and lavish.

"Just a moment, please," the valet said. "Make yourselves comfortable, and I'll let my master know you're here."

He disappeared into a side door, leaving us alone in the space. In the center of the room, leather armchairs were arranged around a large chest that served as something of a table; a carafe of wine and three glasses sat waiting, but neither Pryce nor I availed ourselves. Instead, we took the opportunity to explore. A plush carpet muted our footsteps as we moved from wall to wall, taking in tapestries of extraordinary delicacy and beauty. Each of them showed a scene from Folk lore—or, I realized with a start, perhaps history—highlighted in gold and silver thread: the Cauldron of Rebirth's destruction, the Wild Hunt, Arthur drawing Excalibur from the stone. At the far end of the room stood a fireplace flanked by bookshelves. As I got closer, I saw that one set of shelves held ancient books heavily worked in gold and gems, a few bearing a script I did not recognize. I had never before seen their like, but it was easy to determine that they were Folk in origin. The other side held a few old, embellished books on the upper shelves, but the tomes became more modern and commonplace as they descended, and the titles on the spines were written in English. All of these were about the Folk—as humans saw them. These books spanned hundreds of years, from the 15th century when interactions between Folk and humans were still prevalent, through the first schism, and into the 19th century, including accounts of the victory at Waterloo and beyond.

Pryce stepped up beside me, taking in the display.

"Odd, isn't it?" I said. "That he should have so many human works, if he is one of the voices advocating for a second withdrawal?"

"Know thine enemy," Pryce murmured solemnly. I was robbed of any chance to respond by the sound of a door opening.

As we turned, our host strode into the room. I had seen Lord Evrain on multiple occasions at this point, but only briefly and from afar; this was the first time I'd gotten a good look up close. He approached us confidently, light from the window catching the gold in his hair and giving it the look of a halo. Indeed, there was an air about him of a Renaissance angel, but more Michelangelo than Botticelli. Fine-featured and golden-haired, he was also powerfully built, his musculature clearly defined by his expertly tailored attire. As he reached us, he smiled.

"Gentlemen," he said. "So good of you to accept my invitation. Please, have a seat."

The three of us settled into the armchairs, and the valet stepped forward to take the carafe on the trunk in hand.

"May I offer you some wine?" Lord Evrain said. "It's an excellent vintage—one of the last of my store from the Home Lands."

"No, thank you," Pryce said flatly. "We are on duty."

Lord Evrain's luster seemed to dull a bit. "Of course," he said, and nodded to the valet who poured a single cup, then withdrew to give us privacy.

Lord Evarin took a leisurely sip of his wine, giving us an appraising look over the rim. He was playing a waiting game, refusing to fill the quiet in order to see if we would feign ignorance for the reason of our summons or otherwise prevaricate. I knew it, and I suspect Pryce did too, but he was evidently not in the mood for such pretense.

"May I inquire as to the purpose of this meeting, my lord?"

Rather than seeming put out, I thought I saw a glimmer of something like amusement in Lord Evrain's eyes as he leaned forward to set his glass on the trunk.

"It has come to my attention that there was a murder in the British Quarter the night before last, and that the two of you have been charged with the investigation on the diplomatic end."

I felt Pryce stiffen next to me as my stomach sank. We had known that word of the murder would reach the highest levels of the court, including the more isolationist factions. But to be singled out by one of the leaders and addressed so pointedly—this did not bode well for us at all.

"We have, my lord," Pryce said, keeping his tone level.

"I'm curious, then," Lord Evrain said. "Why you have not reached out to the castle to share your information. One might suspect the embassy is trying to hide something about this particular incident."

"We have a contact at the castle," Pryce said. "Sir Goodfellow."

Lord Evrain's face hardened. "Sir Goodfellow is but one member of this court. There are protocols to follow for these things; he is not employed in any position that would oversee such a circumstance."

"If I may, my lord," Pryce said. "Neither, as I understand it, are you."

I was surprised and rather impressed by Pryce's equanimity. I have never been good at this type of subtle verbal sparring. Father always said that even if I held my tongue when I was in a temper, he could always read my emotions on my face. But however tense Pryce was on the inside, outwardly, he exuded an impression of serenity.

Lord Evrain, however, did not. "The fact remains," he said tightly. "That your office has failed to communicate with the castle about an affair that potentially poses a threat to the safety of Folk here on the island."

"There has been no sign that any Folk are in danger," Pryce said. "The victim was human, and thus, under our jurisdiction."

Lord Evrain pounced, eyes gleaming. "Was there or was there not graffiti at the site indicating anti-human sentiment?"

Pryce let out a slow breath. "There was. But if anything, that would suggest that the perpetrator was Folk. How would that pose a threat to other Folk? It would seem that the other humans on the island were in danger instead."

Lord Evrain leaned forward. "Captain, we all know that tensions are high now. If one of us was driven to commit a crime against one of yours, how long before the pendulum swings the other way? What if a resident of the Quarter takes it upon themselves to seek retribution? This situation has the potential to escalate very quickly."

"The victim was not one of ours—he was an outsider." Pryce said, a futile deflection even to me, and just as the others had predicted, it did nothing to appease Lord Evrain.

"That only proves my point," Lord Evrain said. "If security is so lax in the Quarter, it puts everyone on the island in danger." He shifted in his seat as Pryce and I stewed. "And there is one more thing that concerns me. I understand that Honoria Sherwood is assisting in the investigation."

It was my turn to stiffen, suddenly alert at the mention of Miss Sherwood, but Pryce fielded the observation with that same poised calm. "She is. Why should that be a problem?"

"She's only a girl," Lord Evrain said, and I hated how this observation echoed my own upon first meeting Miss Sherwood. "It seems misguided at best to allow her into such a sensitive manner in an official capacity. And then there is the issue of her unusual family circumstances…"

"And what are those, my lord?" Pryce said, all innocence. Lord Evrain gave him an unimpressed look.

"Coyness does not suit you, Captain. I only worry that her loyalties may be divided. My priorities are clear, as are yours. I think it is possible that Miss Sherwood's could become muddled."

"But surely all those priorities are the same," I interjected, unable to stay quiet any longer. "To see justice done and temper whatever hostilities exist here on the island in order to maintain peace and camaraderie."

Lord Evrain pursed his lips. "Yes. Yes, of course."

"In that case," Pryce said, shooting me a look as he resumed control of the conversation. "It should ease your mind that a suspect—a human suspect—has been detained in Glastonbury." Considering the holes Miss Sherwood had poked in the supposed validity of the arrest, invoking it was a risk, but it was also effective. At Pryce's statement, Lord Evrain showed a flicker of uncertainty for the first time in the proceedings; whoever his spies were, they hadn't gotten this information to him yet. I suspect Pryce found this reaction profoundly satisfying. I know I did.

"Is that right?" Lord Evrain said, regaining his composure and taking up his glance once more. "Such news strikes me as something you might have shared earlier in the conversation."

Pryce said nothing, turning Lord Evrain's trick from earlier back on him. Again, I thought there was something like amusement or approval in the lord's eyes. *Touche*, they seemed to say. An acknowledgment of a worthy opponent, however grudging.

"And how precisely was that happy resolution achieved?" he said.

"Our colleague, Lieutenant Waddington, followed a lead to its logical end," Pryce replied

Lord Evrain raised his eyebrows. "What, the blond sullen one?"

Pryce sighed. "That would be him."

Lord Evrain did not respond further, only shook his

head in apparent disbelief and sipped his wine. Waddington's ability to acquire such a universally deplorable reputation on the island was truly a marvel, but it was not the main issue at hand.

"So, as you can see, my lord," Pryce said. "You need not trouble yourself any further."

"Yes," Lord Evrain said slowly. "I think I do see." He stared at us for a long moment before putting down his wine glass and getting to his feet.

"Thank you, gentlemen. This meeting has been most illuminating, but I have pressing matters to attend to." Pryce and I rose as well, inclining our heads. "Rhys will show you out."

The discreet valet reappeared and ushered us toward the exit as Lord Evrain crossed to the side door, pulling it closed behind him with a resonant bang.

Once Rhys had left us in the hallway, Pryce and I turned as one and made our retreat.

"That did not go especially well," I said.

Pryce grunted. "No, it did not. He is taking a worryingly keen interest in this murder. Obviously, it's something he could use as ammunition in his dealings with the queen, but to press us for details like that…"

"We need to talk to Goodfellow," I said, and Pryce nodded. Internally, I added, "And Miss Sherwood", but I was oddly reluctant to say it out loud. With effort, I pushed my sense of unease aside and followed Pryce out into the brightly lit bailey.

As we approached the curtain wall, I heard the din of raised voices, and when we reached the gate, I saw that it was Waddington of all people, carrying on a very heated discussion with the guards. He caught sight of us and raised a finger, stabbing the air with great force.

"See?" he said. "They're right there!"

The guard he'd been shouting at turned, face flashing with both annoyance and relief when he saw us. He reached out and opened the gate.

"Have you concluded your business here for the day, gentlemen?"

"We have," Pryce said, and the guard turned back to Waddington.

"There now," he said. "Seems like we've all got what we wanted. You've found your associates, and now all of you can clear out of here and stop bothering those of us who are only trying to do our jobs."

Waddington looked like he was about to say something regrettable, but just then a voice called out "Captain!", and we looked up to see Robin Goodfellow hurrying toward the gate.

"Glad I caught you," he said when he reached us, sounding slightly winded. "I was worried you'd already have gone."

"What is it?" Pryce asked, but any immediate response was cut off by the annoyed guard clearing his throat.

"Begging your pardon, sir," he said to Goodfellow, entirely professional now. "But might I ask if you are going in or out?"

"What?" Goodfellow said, then, glancing around, realized we were blocking the gate. "Oh, yes, so sorry. I think out for the moment."

As a group, we moved across the street to the beginnings of the commercial district, still under the watchful eye of the guards. Waddington glared at them, muttering unseemly things under his breath.

"Waddington," Pryce snapped. "What are you doing here?"

With an expression bordering on a sneer, Waddington

thrust an envelope at Pryce. "Message came for you. Said it was urgent."

"And *you* brought it?" Pryce said, opening the message. "As I recall, you didn't seem to fancy heading up this way today."

"The colonel came in after you left," Waddington said peevishly. "I was going to send it with a runner, but he said if it was that important, I needed to bring it myself."

As Pryce began reading, Goodfellow turned to me.

"I do apologize," he said. "I've been in meetings all day, and when I got out just now, I heard you were in an audience with Evrain. I knew he'd try to twist this situation to his advantage, but I didn't think he'd be so bold as to bring the two of you here. I went to his chambers at once, but the valet told me you had already departed."

"It's all right," I assured him, just as Pryce let out a long sigh.

"What is it?" Waddington said, obviously curious for all his bluster.

"Miss Sherwood was right, Waddington," Pryce said. "Charpentier is not the man we're looking for."

Waddington scowled. "What? How could you know that?"

Pryce looked up from the message. "Because there's been another murder in Glastonbury. Joseph Stangerson is dead."

Chapter 11

22 March 1881, cont.

WE PROCEEDED DIRECTLY to the dock, hoping to hire transport to Glastonbury. Waddington asserted quite forcefully that his presence was not required for such an errand, but Pryce was having none of it; he snarled that there was no way he was letting Waddington out of his sight and all but frog-marched the man down to the water. The tide was in, but luck was on our side—a merchant with a small boat was just getting ready to return to the mainland and agreed to let us ride along for a few coins. Pryce sat near the helm, making small talk with the merchant as we set off, while Waddington sequestered himself at the far end of the stern, glowering out at the water. That left Goodfellow and I together in between.

"You're handling this all quite well," he said suddenly.

I shifted to face him. "Sorry?"

"All his 'foul and most unnatural murder'," he said

wryly. "It can't be what you imagined you'd be dealing with upon your arrival."

I chuckled. "No, I suppose not."

"I appreciate it. What you and Pryce have done." I noted that he did not mention Waddington. "These are perilous times. Perhaps the worst I've seen since we've returned to the World of Men."

His face was solemn, nothing like the spritely Puck toying with the hearts of foolish mortals. He looked as if he carried the weight of the world.

"Why is it so important to you?" I said. "Maintaining relations between our people?" I didn't mean it as a challenge; I was genuinely curious.

He was quiet a moment, thinking. When he spoke, his words were not what I expected.

"All the Folk here are so young, doctor." He gave a small humorless laugh at my expression. "I know, it must not seem that way to you, but they are." He sobered again. "None of them remember what it was like in the old days. The others like me, who'd had a life among humans before the first schism—most of them were invited to come back and serve in Mab's court here, but..." He shook his head. "Almost to a one they declined. Some were still loyal to Titania and thought it would sully her memory to return. For others, the experience of breaking ties once was too painful. They weren't willing to risk the possibility of having to do it again."

"But you came." I said, and he nodded.

"I did."

"You didn't feel disloyal?"

"No. You see, what many don't understand, human and Folk alike, is that bringing us back together, and keeping us there, is of a piece with Titania's decision, not a rebuke to it. The World of Men... well, in the years after

Elizabeth's death, it seemed to change. In many ways, it became darker and more dangerous place. I'm not trying to suggest it was ever a carefree idyll, you understand, but the stridency that developed, the wars of religion and conquest – they demonstrated a worldview that was increasingly distant from our own. It was terrifying.

"Titania could be an arrogant hoyden, and she did not suffer fools, whatever your playwrights had to say about it. But she was shrewd, and she knew that if humans, and even some of our own kind, lost sight of one key truth, we were doomed. And that looked likely, so she led us into seclusion to spare us that fate."

"What was the truth?" I said.

"That all of us are poorer when our peoples are at odds. Folk, humans—all of us are bound by our history, by our connection to this land. Arthur knew it. Mab knows it, too. But there are so many voices trying to convince her otherwise."

He fell quiet again, watching the beach bob closer. I wondered if he felt he'd said too much and would retreat into that safety of formality and silence. But after a moment, he spoke again.

"Our lives are long. We see so much change in the human world in the space of just one of our generations, and we see it over and over again. But even for us, the recent years have seemed turbulent. Napoleon was only the beginning of this new wave. Whatever challenges the future holds, we will be better able to face them together. Cavendish may be a pompous ass, but he has one thing right—our fates are intertwined. And withdrawing to the Home Lands may work for a while—a long while even—but with all the terrible and wonderful marvels your kind has produced, we can't count on hiding forever."

We had reached the shore then, and Pryce and the

merchant hopped out to guide the craft up onto the sand. I had thought my conversation with Goodfellow was over, but as we prepared to disembark, he offered one last observation.

"She holds you in high esteem, you know."

I quirked a brow, confused. "Who, Mab?"

He laughed. "Sorry, no. I'm not privy to her opinion of you." He let his voice drop, so only I could hear. "Honoria. She does not impress easily, but you have earned her favor."

I thought of her fury that morning and felt skeptical. But Goodfellow seemed sincere; the words even carried a hint of unspoken challenge—an implied *Don't disappoint her*. I had little time to consider it, though, for all of us were then clambering into a wagon to be taken the rest of the way to Glastonbury.

Upon reaching the city, we proceeded to the address indicated in Pryce's message. As we mounted the stairs of the boarding house we found there, the door opened to reveal Miss Sherwood on the threshold. I would have asked how she'd come to be there, but I had already recognized that her innate perspicacity bordered on the occult. Of course she'd been the one to summon us to the scene.

She nodded to Goodfellow, Pryce and I in turn as we reached the top of the stairs; Waddington she ignored entirely, which, all things considered, seemed rather charitable. "Gentlemen," she said. "Right this way."

We followed her down a narrow hallway to a sitting room where two county constables were speaking to a thin, skittish man in wire-framed glasses.

"Constables," Miss Sherwood said as we entered. "These are the officers from the embassy." The constables nodded a greeting, and Miss Sherwood turned to the skittish man. "Mr. Barnaby, could you tell these men the same thing you told us?"

Mr. Barnaby nodded, unconsciously twisting a handkerchief in his fingers. "Well, it was just that we were all up and stirring, getting ready for the day, you know, when we heard the most almighty shriek coming from upstairs. I hurried up there as quick as I could and saw Lucy, our daily girl who had been cleaning the room of our tenant who's just left. She was standing in front of that Mr. Stangerson's room, white as a ghost, with one hand over her mouth and the other pointing at the floor, and when I looked where she was pointing, I saw that a stream of blood had seeped out from under the door and was soaking into the runner there in the hallway."

I glanced at Pryce and saw he was frowning. Both of us, I knew, were remembering the blood that had drenched the scene of Drebber's murder but had not been his. Could the perpetrator be so incompetent as to injure himself twice in the perpetration of his crimes?

"Well," Mr. Barnaby went on. "I sent Lucy for the keys, which I'd left behind in my rush, and when she got back, I opened the door and found Mr. Stangerson there, curled up on the floor stone dead. So, of course, I sent for the constables, and then they arrived, and not long after Miss Sherwood there showed up, and now you gentlemen. And that's all I know."

"Has the crime scene been disturbed?" Pryce asked, and one of the constables shook his head.

"No, sir. We did a cursory examination, but what with the connection to the Drebber case, we wanted to leave it until your people got here."

"Good man," Pryce said with an affirming nod and turned to me. "Shall we?"

I gestured for him to lead the way, then followed him

towards the stairs. Wordlessly, Miss Sherwood, Goodfellow, and, finally, Waddington, fell into step behind me. At the top of the stairs, we all trailed down a narrow hallway and stopped in front of the door where, yes, blood had soaked into the narrow carpet running the length of the corridor. Mr. Barnaby opened the door, and Miss Sherwood and Goodfellow immediately stepped inside, while the rest of us proceeded more slowly. The room was in disarray, clearly the aftermath of a struggle, and the air was freezing, courtesy of an open window. Just as at the scene of the first murder, the word "SAIS" had been scrawled on the wall in blood. The source of the blood was readily apparent: Mr. Stangerson, dressed only in his nightshirt, lay crumpled on the floor amid the tumult with a deep, narrow wound in his left side, the type made by some kind of blade.

"The murderer changed up his method," Pryce observed. "Don't these fellows tend to select one means of killing and adhere to it?"

Miss Sherwood made an affirmative sound as she crouched next to Stangerson's body, brow furrowed as she adjusted her skirts to keep them from trailing in the blood. Her choice of trousers on the night of Drebber's murder suddenly made more sense.

"The window was open when you discovered him?" she asked. A constable who had come upstairs after our little retinue nodded.

"We found a milk boy who said he saw a bloke going down a ladder in the alley just before sunup. We checked, and the ladder is still out there."

Pryce raised his eyebrows.

"The man would have been covered in blood," he said. "Why didn't the boy raise an alarm?"

"Our man is methodical," Goodfellow said from where

he stood near the wall, gazing down into a washbasin sitting on the battered dresser. "He washed up here before he left." The wight lifted his eyes to Pryce and me. "If his skin was clean, and he was wearing a dark suit, it would have been easy enough for him to go unnoticed in the predawn."

Apparently satisfied that she had obtained all the intelligence she could from the body, Miss Sherwood was surveying the room with a look of intense concentration. She began poking delicately around in the mess, drawing out a handful of objects that she quickly discarded as irrelevant—a dime novel with a painted desert on its cover, a pipe, a cracked water glass. Then she paused, eyes suddenly intent. Slowly, she leaned forward and collected a small object from underneath the bed. Sitting back on her heels, she held the object up, revealing that it was a small enamel box, its top bearing an inlaid image of balanced scales. As we watched, she eased the box open and stared down at its contents, her face taking on an expression of quiet triumph.

"Eureka," she murmured.

Reaching into the box, she retrieved a small, vaguely spherical object that gleamed gold when she held it up to the light from the window. I recognized it immediately, though I had only encountered its like on one or two earlier occasions, and its presence here cast a new and interesting light on Drebber's probable cause of death.

"What is it?" said Pryce.

"A pill," Miss Sherwood said, returning the object in question to the box and snapping the lid shut. "Opium, if I'm not mistaken."

"Opium? How do you figure?"

Miss Sherwood pushed herself to her feet, brushing off her skirt with her free hand. "Even in death, Mr. Drebber's countenance did not show marked signs of physical or emotional distress. If he'd been poisoned—and I believed he had—it was not by anything that would cause pain or visible trauma to the body. That suggested some type of narcotic to me, likely one that is commonly used for recreational purposes, and when I checked his eyes, his pupils had shrunk to pinpoints, which is consistent with opium overdose."

"Well, that's all fine and good," said Waddington, somehow thinking his input would be useful or welcome. "But how does that help us find the killer?" I rolled my eyes at his use of the word "us".

"It doesn't," Miss Sherwood said, finally acknowledging him. "But it gives us a more complete picture of his frame of mind."

"Hang his frame of mind!" Waddington shouted. I found myself taking a step forward, closer to Miss Sherwood. "We need to find him before he murders again!"

She stared at him without flinching, her face a picture of equanimity, though her eyes were fierce.

"The odds of that happening would be significantly higher if all of us had spent the afternoon following evidence rather than sulking at our desks."

Waddington's face went nearly purple with rage. He opened his mouth a few times, but couldn't seem to settle on anything in particular to say. Eventually, he gave up and shoved past Pryce, storming into the hallway. The county constables looked at each other uncertainly, probably questioning why they were even there. Goodfellow stepped up to Miss Sherwood's side.

"What are you thinking, my dear?"

"I think," she said. "That we should go find a cab."

The constables looking dubious regarding this rather arbitrary turn in the conversation, but it gave them an excuse to leave, which they rapidly took. Miss Sherwood handed the box to Goodfellow, who tucked it into an interior jacket pocket, and the four of us made our way back downstairs.

On the ground floor, Pryce conferred with the remaining constables and told Mr. Barnaby that someone would be along to collect the body so he could set about cleaning the room. We found Waddington out on the front porch smoking a cigarette, and, as luck would have it, an empty cab was waiting at the curb. Pryce hailed the cabman and looked to Miss Sherwood.

"And where is it exactly that we're going?"

"Well," Miss Sherwood said thoughtfully, as the cabman came around to open the door for her. "I'm not sure we need to go very far at all to bring this investigation to its conclusion. Wouldn't you agree, Mr. Hope?"

Even as we all turned to face her, baffled by this non sequitur, I felt the cabman go rigid next to me, and when I glanced over, I saw that all the blood had drained from his face. His eyes met mine for a fraction of a second, a pall of understanding settling in them, and then he made to bolt. He was a tall man and quick, but his moment of surprised hesitation proved his undoing. Pryce and I were able to tackle him, wrestling him to the ground even as he struggled and fought. His face was in the dirt, breath coming fast and arms twisted up behind his back before he went slack, like a puppet with its strings cut—unconscious. Still, Pryce and I remained vigilant, moving by unspoken agreement to crouch on either side of him. A shadow fell over us, and when I looked up, Miss Sherwood stood there.

"Gentlemen," she said. "Behold our murderer."

Chapter 12

22 March 1881, cont.

WITH SOME GRUDGING assistance from Waddington, we were able to lift the man and carry him inside. Mr. Barnaby permitted us the use of a ground level room, perhaps not entirely from the kindness of his heart—it couldn't have been good for business to have an unconscious man laid out in the lobby. We settled the man in question on the bed, then stood gazing down at his unmoving form.

"What precisely just happened?" Pryce said, with perhaps a touch less of his usual implacable calm.

"When our man wakes up," said Miss Sherwood. "You'll find that he is a Mr. Geoffrey Hope, former human resident of Ynis Witrin and self-appointed angel of vengeance for a sylph by the name of Marina, who once a paramour of Drebber's."

We all stared at her, nonplussed. I'm sure she would have been pelted with questions directly, only just then, the man in the bed groaned.

His eyes fluttered open, and he looked around. I could see the moment he realized where he was, for his pale face took on a look of resignation as he sighed, letting his head sink deeper into the pillow.

"Well, I had hoped it wouldn't come to this," he said. "But I can't say I'm surprised."

"Is your name Geoffrey Hope?" said Pryce. "And are you responsible for the murders of Lieutenant Enoch Drebber and Mr. Joseph Stangerson?"

"It is, and I am," he replied, his voice calm and even.

Pryce's eyebrows shot up. I don't think any of us had been expecting such a ready admission.

"You do realize that anything you say to use can be used against you when you're brought before the magistrate?" said Pryce.

The man shrugged. "It doesn't matter now. What's done is done, and my time on this earth is nearing its end, whatever happens in the courts."

The mood in the room shifted to one of alarm, and he chuckled.

"Oh, don't act so shocked. I'm not seeking to end my life." He turned his gaze to me. "Am I correct in understanding you're a doctor?"

I nodded.

"Then put your hand here," he said, motioning to his chest. "I think it will clarify some things."

I did as he asked and immediately noticed a powerful, unusual throbbing. Something seemed to rattle inside his chest cavity, and in the room's quiet, I could hear a wheeze I had not noticed before.

I stared at him, wide-eyed.

"You have an aortic aneurysm."

"I do," he confirmed. "It's not new, but it has worsened

recently. I saw a doctor last week about it, and he told me that it is bound to burst before long. I had hoped to spend my last days in peace, but I have sowed my field, and now, I suppose, I will need to reap it."

"Is what he says true?" Pryce asked me. "Is his life in danger?

"Definitely," I answered. "Though it is hard to tell any more without my medical bag."

Miss Sherwood had not taken her eyes off of Hope at any time during this exchange. Now, she pulled up a nearby chair and sat near the head of the bed.

"Are you ready to make your full confession, Mr. Hope?" she said.

He cast her a bemused look. "And are you to be my priest? Offer me absolution?"

"If you like," she said, and he snorted.

"I'm not sure it would take. I don't regret what I've done."

"Tell us anyway," Miss Sherwood said. Hope cocked his head, considering her.

"All right," he said after a long beat. "I'll tell you."

"I was just a little thing when my mother got a job on the island—one of the good ones at the castle that included room and board. My father had died at sea, and it was a fine situation for a widow with a young son, even if it was among the Folk. When I was old enough, I went to the island school, which was a misery. Mama always said that I had just as much right to be there as anyone, but it was obvious that nobody else agreed. Children and adults alike went out of their way to remind me of my place, as if I could forget.

"It was only with Linetta and Marina that I felt something like peace. We were of a similar age, relatively speaking, and their mother worked at the castle like mine. We were thick as thieves, always playing games of exploring the island together. Sometimes, when the weather was nice, we would run down the causeway while the tide was out, spending hours in the hills by the sea.

"I loved both of them dearly, but over time, I came to realize that my feelings for Marina were changing. Linetta was like a sister to me, but my heart was drawn to Marina the way they talk about in stories. I was falling in love with her.

"It was a hopeless desire; I knew that. Courtship between our kind and the Folk simply wasn't done—It was something forbidden, something wicked." He blanched, face coloring as he glanced at Miss Sherwood. "Begging your pardon, miss." She held up a mollifying hand, gesturing for him to continue. "I understood that there could be no intimacy between us, even if Marina had returned my feelings, which I was far from sure of. I had accepted that I was destined to love her from afar and decided it was enough." His face darkened, jaw hardening. "And then Drebber came."

Pryce frowned. "He wasn't stationed at Ynis Witrin. There would have been a record of it."

"No," Hope said. "But he was friends with some that were. He would visit from time to time—carouse, get up to mischief."

"But wouldn't that have been when Lord Warford was still in charge?" I said. "I thought the feeling on the island was calmer then."

"It was," Hope said. "But that didn't mean there wasn't ever trouble. And Drebber *was* trouble, though Marina couldn't see it. She was smitten from the moment she laid eyes on him. He was handsome, charming, quick to laugh. Honestly, he could have had his pick of girls, but for some reason, he chose her. He'd pop up where he knew she'd be, give her little notes and gifts. I tried to deny the bad feeling I had about him. I thought it was just jealousy, and I wanted her to be happy, even if it wasn't with me. But I knew she was in trouble when he gave her that ring— poppies, because they were her favorite."

"An interesting choice, the poppy," Miss Sherwood cut in. "Scientific name: papaver somniferum. Commonly associated with fertility deities in the ancient world. It was ascribed to Demeter in ancient Greece, as goddess of the harvest, and Morpheus, god of dreams—but also to Thanatos, the god of death."

Hope gave a humorless laugh. "Well, that's not too far off the mark, as it turned out. But I'm getting ahead of myself. Marina thought Drebber loved her. She thought he was going to marry her. And he let her believe it because it suited his purpose.

"He told her that if she came to England to meet his family, she'd be able to win them over, even with her being one of the Folk. She wanted to talk to her mum about it, but he said, no, it needed to be a secret for the time being. He said he'd go the family estate first, then Stangerson would bring her along later. It was all arranged. And she never breathed a word of it to any of us. One day, she was just gone."

He paused, shifting uncomfortably. "Can I get a glass of water? This talking is making my mouth dry." Pryce procured one for him and he drank deeply, closing his eyes to collect himself for a moment. When he opened them again, he nodded, ready to continue.

"You can probably see where this is going. Stangerson took her to the country house, but the family was not there —it was only Drebber, who seduced her, then left while she was sleeping. She came home days later, heartsick and, we discovered later, expecting. We all did what we could to keep her spirits up, let her know she wouldn't have to deal with this alone, but she was just a shell of who she'd been before. Drebber had stolen the most essential part of her."

He paused, looking down at his hands. In the low light, I saw his lip tremble.

"The birth ended up being too much for her to bear. Based on what Linetta told me, they just couldn't stop the bleeding. By the time the night was over, she was gone. And then the babe followed her."

The room was deathly silent. A pindrop would have sounded like a thunderclap.

"I was sick with grief and fury, but I couldn't show it to my mother, couldn't even show it to Linetta. So I swallowed it down inside of me, but rather than shrinking in the darkness, it festered, turning ugly and heavy. Every day, it became more of a burden, surrounded as I was by reminders of her. And so, finally, I could take it no longer. I packed my things, took that cursed ring with me as a memento of what I'd lost, and ran."

"London seemed an easy place to get lost in, so that's where I went. We never had many horses on the island, but I'd always been good with them, so I got a job at a stable, and from there I started driving a cab. But I couldn't escape the pain. I started drinking away my pay, and when that didn't work anymore..."

"You took to opium," Miss Sherwood finished.

He nodded, smiling grimly. "I thought there was a certain poetry to that—that the poppy would be the downfall of us both."

"But it wasn't your downfall," Miss Sherwood said. "At least, not at first."

"No," Hope said. "I passed out on my way home one night and woke up in one of the hospitals run by church groups out to save those of us drawn to the pipe. They'd found me half dead in the streets and were determined to set me right. I didn't make it easy for them, but eventually, they won me over. I decided to quit. I wanted my health and my life back. So I started life in London over, deciding I would do it without intoxicants this time."

"Except snuff," Miss Sherwood cut in.

Pryce raised his eyebrows. "Snuff? Really?"

Hope dipped his chin, looking sheepish.

"I know it's old-fashioned," he said. "But it's also unobtrusive. Especially in those early days when I was worried about backsliding, it allowed me to partake frequently without attracting attention or offending sensibilities. Helped soothe my nerves.

"Anyway, I thought I'd put the whole affair of Marina and Drebber behind me. I'd been diagnosed with the aneurysm then—the cost of too much hard living—but it was stable. I was working again. And then Linetta wrote to tell me that Drebber had returned. As soon as I got her message, I dropped everything and came back.

"In fairly short order, I discovered Drebber was not on active duty. Rather, he had been seconded out of his regiment and was, for all practical purposes, free to pursue whatever struck his fancy, which was apparently taking rooms in the city so he could carouse with friends of his who were stationed nearby—and those who were still employed by the embassy.

"I was obsessed with pursuing Drebber, but I also needed coin to feed and house myself in town; happily, taking up my familiar role as a cabman accomplished both of those things. I tracked Drebber and Stangerson through Glastonbury and its environs, taking note of where they spent their time and with whom. But whenever they accompanied embassy associates onto the island, I could not follow."

"Wait," I said. "If he had been spending time on the island, how did none of us recognize him? I would swear that before I examined his corpse, I had never seen the man before in my life."

"I suspect that Drebber frequented gatherings of a rather more intimate nature than we typically attend," Pryce said.

Hope scowled. "You could say that. Anyway, in my cabman role, I was far too conspicuous. I needed a way to move around on the island without attracting attention, and Drebber typically ventured into the tor for evening entertainments, so making myself an honorary member of the constabulary's nightly patrol seemed ideal."

Pryce made a noise of incredulity. "And by 'honorary member', you mean 'complete and utter fraud'."

Hope shrugged. "It was easy enough to piece together a passable copy of the uniform. After that, it was only a matter of strolling around with a sense of purpose in the dark, which still allowed me to drive my cab during the day. But it turned out that following Drebber to Ynis Witrin didn't solve my biggest problem. Whatever side of the tor he was on, he was never alone. He was always with a group of intimates or a conquest or, at the very least, Stangerson. I was beginning to despair of ever isolating him enough to seek my vengeance. But then, one day, I finally had a stroke of luck.

"I saw Mr. Charpentier chase Drebber out of his boarding house, and when the weeping sister followed hot on their heels, it wasn't hard to figure out what he'd done, the blackguard. I trailed them at a reasonable distance, and eventually, I saw Drebber break away from Charpentier, who followed for a bit, but then seemed to decide Drebber wasn't worth it. He collected himself and wandered off I know not where—it was no concern of mine. Drebber was alone, and it seemed I would finally have my chance.

"I lost him, briefly, but then caught sight of him again, just as he was stumbling into a gin palace. I didn't want to follow him in—too many people, too much chance of discovery—but I parked my cab at the curb, and I waited. It was hours, and still I waited, turning down fares whenever anyone tried to hire me, and some of them were less than charitable about the refusal, let me tell you. Anyway, finally—finally—Drebber came out, completely scammered, with his arm around another fellow who was far worse for drink, singing some bawdy song. I had not anticipated this new friend, but after so much time, I would not let this opportunity pass me by. I called out to them, asking if they needed a ride, and after some discussion, most of which was complete gibberish, the two of them piled into the cab.

"I'd had plenty of time to think while I was sitting out there waiting on him, and I had decided that it would be best for me to take him back to Ynis Witrin to do the deed. As a cabman, I know Glastonbury uncommonly well, but as a constable, I'd gotten to know every inch of the Quarter. I knew the cottages would be deserted, and even unfinished, wrapped up in tarps as they were, they'd keep us hidden from prying eyes. With this in mind, I made straight for the tor. Once I was through the tunnel, I parked the cab near the road just off the beach. When I opened the cab door, I saw that both of them had passed out, which was actually a boon. I roused Drebber, who was still so soused that he didn't notice where we were. I left the other bloke in the cab and set about hauling Drebber across the causeway.

"And nothing stopped you?" said Waddington. "Not the enchantment, not the sentries, nothing?"

With a wry grin, Hope reached into his shirt and pulled out a token. "I may have been gone awhile, but I am still one of Ynis Witrin's own. And as for the sentries—Drebber was drunk, but he wasn't struggling; there was nothing in his behavior to suggest he was with me against his will. And I didn't have any malicious intent regarding the castle or even the island, so why would they have taken note of me?

"Anyway, it was an ordeal, but we did finally make it to the cottage. By this time, Drebber was sobering up a bit. He looked around the empty house, confused, and turned to me. I asked if he remembered me, and when he said nothing, I brought out the ring and asked if he remembered Marina. If he ever thought about their child. He claimed he knew nothing of the child, which could very well have been true. I had sought to inform Drebber, but the letters presumably went to Stangerson first, and who knows what he did with them. It doesn't really matter; the ending was the same.

"Drebber became enraged and lunged at me. I was able to overpower him easily enough—he spent the little strength and energy he had in that first burst of anger—but he managed a good punch to my nose in the struggle, which is why there was blood everywhere. He was practically in tears at that point and asked if I was going to shoot him. But no, that would have been too easy. Instead, I told him to choose a pill from my box."

"The opium," Miss Sherwood said, and he nodded.

"I'd gotten a bloke I knew from my days of skulking around opium dens to make them for me. Drebber would answer to the poppy that he'd used to hurt Marina. Like, I said—poetry. I did give him a fair shot. One pill of the two was harmless; if Providence saw fit to give him another chance, so be it. But if not... he would finally pay for what he'd done."

Pryce and I shared a look. I couldn't tell if Hope genuinely believed in this flawed logic, or if it was just something he told himself to justify his actions. Ultimately, the distinction probably meant little.

"Well, he hemmed and hawed, but he finally made his choice. He drifted off fairly quickly, but I wasn't sure the drug would be enough to truly end things. So I waited. I waited for hours. Until finally, he stopped breathing. I checked his pulse, just to be sure. And then I left."

"Hold on," Pryce said. "What was that business with 'sais' on the wall?"

Again, Hope looked sheepish.

"Seemed like a good idea at the time. Thought it might throw people like you off my scent."

"You don't seem particularly concerned about getting caught now that it's happened," Waddington said. "What changed between then and now?"

"Like, I said when I woke up—I had hoped it wouldn't come to this. What's done is done. I would have preferred spending my last days eating good food and drinking good wine, saying goodbye to the ones I care about."

"You weren't eating good food and drinking good wine last night," Pryce pointed out. "You were out killing Stangerson. Even though it seemed as if you'd gotten off scot free for murder." All eyes turned to Waddington, who seemed to wither a bit.

"Convenient," Goodfellow observed blandly. "That an alternate suspect was so close at hand."

"Are you tangled up in this somehow?" Pryce asked, glaring daggers at Waddington. "Did you frame Charpentier to cover your own misdeeds?"

"No!" Waddington burst out, getting back a bit of his

bravado. "I swear it. Everything I told you about tracking him to the boarding house was true. I honestly believed Charpentier was guilty."

"But there is more to your involvement in this state of affairs than you let on," Miss Sherwood said. "Isn't there?"

Waddington rounded on her, as if to argue, but she locked eyes with him and refused to look away. Eventually, he slumped, running a hand over his face and hair. Then he turned his attention back to the room at large and began to speak.

"Drebber and I... well, we weren't what you'd call friends, but we'd known each other for years. Our families were acquainted, and we traveled in common circles. About 18 months ago, we found ourselves at the same hunting party; it was the beginning of pheasant season. The host had invited a large group of chaps to attend— old school friends, some of the younger gentry who had taken their seats in Parliament, that sort of thing. Well, you know how it goes with events like that." He paused, waiting for agreement, though none of us in the room actually did know. "After dinner one night, we started playing billiards and broke out the host's store of whiskey. Then all of us proceeded to get very, very drunk.

"While we were imbibing, we started swapping stories of conquests, and Drebber—" He cut himself off, looking pained, but then took a breath and continued. "Drebber started making vulgar insinuations about one of the other bloke's sisters." Pryce swore under his breath, and on the bed, Hope snorted in disgust. "Some of us tried to intervene and diffuse the tension, but one thing led to another, and this bloke—Charlton—called Drebber out."

"Oh, for pity's sake," I muttered. This story was growing more preposterous by the moment. It's been decades since quarrels were regularly settled with pistols at dawn. "What on earth was the man thinking?"

Waddington shrugged. "As I said, we'd all had quite a lot of whiskey. Anyway, Drebber accepted the challenge, and various factions split off to prepare for the event. Dawn was only a few hours away, so there wasn't much time. Our host furnished the pistols, and one of the other guests sent for a doctor, but Drebber was left scrambling for a second. That toady Stangerson would normally have been the one to do it, but he was visiting family nearby or somesuch. So Drebber declared it should be me."

"You?" Pryce said, incredulous. "You served as a second in an actual duel?"

Waddington sighed. "If only. As the sun was rising, we all staggered out to the clearing that had been selected as the arena, so to speak. Most of us still hadn't sobered up, despite the liberal intake of coffee, so when the time came to load and check the pistols, something—I'm still not entirely sure what—went wrong. Drebber accidentally shot Charlton in the thigh." He swallowed, face going grey at the memory. "It happened so quickly; there was blood everywhere. Someone finally had the presence of mind to attempt a tourniquet, but it was too late. When the doctor arrived, he said the bullet had struck the femoral artery."

My stomach went cold in sympathetic horror. It must have been a terrifying, chaotic way to die.

"Well, as you can imagine, that sobered all of us up right quick. We knew if word got out, Drebber would go down for murder, and the rest of us wouldn't fare particularly well, either. So our host came up with an idea—we would take the body to the road and stage it to appear as if he'd been set upon by highwaymen."

There were deep sighs of exasperation throughout the room.

"Waddington, really," Pryce said. "I've seen Christmas pantos less ridiculous than this story."

"It wasn't my idea," Waddington protested, but his heart wasn't in it. "In any case, we didn't have any other real options to speak of. After some debate, we all agreed to the plan. We took Charlton out to the road, threw some of his belongings about, and left hoofprints in the mud. Then we all swore to never speak of it again."

"What of the doctor?" I said.

"Our host paid him off," Waddington replied, and I resolved to follow up on *that* piece of information at some point in the future.

"So then what happened?" asked Pryce.

"At first nothing," Waddington said. "We all packed up and went our separate ways. But somebody cracked. Word got out. Not widely—it was all whispers and insinuations. But one of those whispers made it to my father.

"He was livid, of course, but he came through for me in the end, just like he always has." I rather thought that explained a good bit of what was wrong with Waddington, but I kept that observation to myself. "He arranged for me to be separated from the regiment and moved to a more remote location where I would be less likely to become embroiled in any scandal."

"And that's when you came here," Pryce said grimly.

"And why you reacted as you did when you heard Drebber's name," I put in.

"And it's ultimately why you wanted to find Drebber's killer," Pryce continued. "There was no concern about justice or what the colonel thought of your performance."

"Well, the colonel actually did say all those things I told you," Waddington said. Because of course he did. "But that wasn't the main reason. It was because..." His voice trailed off, as if he couldn't bear to say the next part aloud.

"Because if Drebber had been killed in retribution for the duel, you could be next," Miss Sherwood said.

Waddington nodded miserably.

Pryce sighed, giving Waddington a look of disgust. "Well, as abhorrent as all of this is," he said, turning back to Hope. "It still brings us back around to the fact that Waddington had found what seemed to be a solid suspect. You were in the clear. You could have walked away without a backward glance and, as you said, spent your last days wining and dining. So why didn't you?"

Hope looked almost pleading.

"Don't you see?" Hope said, turning his palms up in a gesture of futility. "He was in it up to his neck, too. He helped Drebber every step of the way. The job wouldn't be done—justice wouldn't be done—until he was gone, too."

"But it didn't go to plan, did it?" Miss Sherwood said. "Stangerson didn't cooperate like Drebber did."

"No," Hope said, sounding regretful. "It took some legwork to track him down. He'd bolted from Charpentier's once he found out about Drebber; I was worried he might have left the city. But he was too much of a coward to go far. That's why it surprised me when he wouldn't stay down, once I was finally in the room with him. I didn't even mean to bring the knife with me; it's just a habit keeping it on me. It was the only way I could get him to stop making a fuss."

"One last thing," I said. "What was Linetta's involvement? Were you working together?"

He shook his head, his face showing something like shame for the first time that night.

"No—please don't place any blame on her. That fool of a constable distracted me when I was trying to make my escape, and I didn't realize I'd left the ring behind until later. I was heartsick—it was the last bit of Marina I had left. In the morning, I went to Linetta and explained what happened. She was furious. I think she was tempted to turn me in herself. But Marina was her sister. She wanted the ring back, too. When she heard that someone had found it, she took it upon herself to go claim it, but that was the extent of her involvement. Truly. She is not to blame for any of this."

"The ring she claimed is not the real one," I said, and he nodded.

"I know. I was able to tell as soon as I saw it." He looked from me to Miss Sherwood. "I think Linetta would like the real one back. Now that this is over."

"We'll get it to her," Miss Sherwood said.

Hope fell quiet then. Having unburdened himself, he now looked wan and depleted.

"I think that's everything," he said finally. "I'm not sorry for what I did. I would do it again. And that's all I have to say." He closed his eyes, either intent on sleep or wanting us to think he was, and sighed, settling deeper into the mattress. Moved by some unspoken signal, Goodfellow, Pryce, and Waddington moved to the far side of the room to confer about what to do next. Miss Sherwood got to her feet, smoothing her skirts, but she did not join them.

"I need some air," she said and left the room. After a moment, I followed her.

It was full dark by then. Miss Sherwood's stood at the porch railing, her arms crossed over her chest and eyes straight ahead. She didn't seem herself.

"Are you all right?" I said quietly.

"No," she replied, and a tear slid down her cheek. She did not wipe it away.

"Some of the things he said were quite shocking," I said, feeling clumsy in my attempt at comfort, and she made a sound of impatience.

"I am not shocked. I am *sad*. Drebber ruined every single thing he touched. Lives wasted. So much pain." She shook her head mournfully.

I watched her profile, touched by the depth of her compassion. That was the key to her, I could see now. She wasn't trying to meddle with her endless questions and her schemes, not seeking recognition or accolades for her cleverness. She was trying to restore something broken to wholeness. I had sensed it before, but now I was able to put words to it. I cleared my throat.

"About earlier," I said haltingly. "What I said was... well, it was bad form. I'm sorry."

"I know," she replied, and there was no triumph in her voice, or dismissal. It was a simple, factual acknowledgment. I almost laughed, and, encouraged by a response that was not a flat-out dismissal, I took a step closer.

"How did you know? About Hope?"

She sighed, raising a hand to massage the back of her neck. "Before I left for that insipid ball last night, I enjoined Mary to ask around among the servants to see if anyone had information on this Linetta. By the time I got home, she had discovered the rough outlines of the tale Mr. Hope told us just now."

I raised my eyebrows. "She works fast."

Miss Sherwood smiled. "Yes, she is a most valued associate in possession of a rare mind. The version of the story she handed off to me was vague in some particulars, flat out wrong in others—Mary was told that Marina's heartbroken swain was named Haines, or possibly Hartwell —but it was something to work with. I took it upon myself to reach out to a handful of friendly human acquaintances here on the island to see if the story rang any bells for them, which it did. Then one of them told me something interesting. He said that while Mr. Hope had absented himself to London some time ago, he thought he'd seen the man driving a cab in Glastonbury just last week.

"The story was coming together, but I checked with one of the sentries on duty that night, just to be sure. As I predicted, he told me that a cab had been spotted coming through the tunnel near Drebber's supposed time of death. Taking all of this information into account along with the story recounted by Constable Rance, I suspected something along the lines of the double life Mr. Hope described to us—cabman by day, constable by night. When I arrived in Glastonbury to gather more information and came upon the second crime scene, I sent a boy to the office of the nearest cab company with a request for Mr. Hope to come to the boarding house for a job. When we walked outside and I took in his appearance— tall and ruddy-faced, with round-toed boots and long fingernails, just as I'd expected—I knew we had our man."

I nodded, struck once again by her mental dexterity. "Well, I'm glad it's settled. I wonder what will transpire regarding Drebber now."

She turned to look at me for the first time. "What do you mean?"

"Well, he may not have deserved to be murdered, but he committed a great wrong—well, multiple wrongs, but most pressing for us, he treated a girl of the Folk abominably, leading to her eventual death. Something should be done on her behalf. Justice needs to be done in her name."

She stared at me. "And what would that look like?"

"Sorry?"

"Would they give Drebber a posthumous discharge with ignominy? Court martial his corpse? Is that how these things work?"

"Well, no, but—"

"Nothing is going to be done about Drebber. Hope's justice is all Marina is going to get."

I felt a catch in my chest. "You really believe that?"

"Yes," she said. "I am genuinely flummoxed that you don't."

I stared at her for a moment, some unidentifiable emotion churning inside me, then stalked across the porch to the opposite railing, leaning on it and gazing into the night. After a moment, Miss Sherwood came to join me.

"Please understand," she said. "I do not intend to cause you pain. But you must see that I am right."

And perhaps I did, but I did not want to. I kept my eyes straight ahead, refusing to answer.

"Do you know where it came from?" she said finally. "My hunger to learn everything I could about... well, everything?"

Still, I said nothing, but I nor did I stop her, so she continued.

"Understanding of the science behind miscegenation between Folk and humans is incomplete. Our biological inheritance can manifest itself in a variety of different ways. It presented the same way in my sister and me, presumably because we are identical twins. We can see glamour, and even manipulate it, though to a lesser extent than the offspring of two Folk parents. But we cannot tell when people are lying." I looked up as she met my eyes. "That terrified me as a child, as much when we were with my father's family in Yorkshire as when we were here. Perhaps moreso—since humans don't have glamour to lean on, they are much more cunning in their deployment of deceit. It still terrifies me. I want to make the world more honest. But I have to start by being honest about how it is now."

I looked at her, turning her words over in my head. I

was humbled and almost unbearably touched by her gentleness. But I couldn't concede her point. I just couldn't.

Goodfellow and Waddington came out onto the porch then, and we turned to face them.

"We decided he should remain here tonight," Goodfellow said. "Pryce is staying with him. We'll reevaluate in the morning." I nodded. "Miss Sherwood has a carriage waiting from earlier, if I am not mistaken. Can we give you and Lieutenant Waddington a ride back?"

I could see Waddington about to accept, but he was too slow.

"No," I said quickly, ignoring Waddington's squawk of protest. "We can make our own way, thank you."

Goodfellow gave me an unreadable look. "Very well then. Safe travels."

"Good night, Dr. Jarvis," I heard Miss Sherwood say as we turned to go.

"Good night, Miss Sherwood," I said over my shoulder. I found I could not face her properly.

And then I went down the front steps to actually hire a cab.

I fear I have made a terrible muck of things, but I find that even now, I'm having difficulty reconciling myself to the things Miss Sherwood said on the porch. And more than that, I am unsure why this inability is causing me such turmoil. I suppose it could be because since meeting Miss Sherwood, I have had a sense of something like purpose again, like clarity, and now that all feels tainted. Specious. Perhaps she is not what I imagined.

I am weary, and it is late. I think I shall retire before I succumb to a dismal malaise.

Your brother,
Wilf

Chapter 13

23 March 1881

DEAR ESTHER,

I did not sleep well last night. Around dawn, I gave up tossing and turning and got out of bed. I took my time getting ready and breaking my fast, but it was still quite early when I arrived at the office. I expected the place to be empty, but to my surprise, Colonel Abercrombie was there. As I made my way through the reception area, I heard him call out from his office.

"Doctor? Is that you?"

"Yes, sir," I called back.

"Come in here. I'd like to talk to you."

I did as he requested, coming to a stop before his desk.

"How did you know it was me, sir?"

"I know Pryce is in town, and Waddington sounds like an intoxicated horse when he walks. You were the only option left." I fought a smile.

"It seems you had quite the night," he continued.

"Sir?" I said. I couldn't conceive how he would have known that, not so early in the morning. He reached into a desk drawer and withdrew a file, which he dropped on his desk with a solid thwack.

"Pryce spent his vigil writing up a report for me," he said, looking half impressed, half stupefied. "Had it messengered to my house before sunrise."

"That does seem in keeping with his general character," I said, and the colonel chuckled.

"So it does," he said. "I also received word from the county magistrate that Mr. Charpentier has been released as a result of Mr. Hope's confession."

"Did he give a reason for his unwillingness to offer a convincing alibi?"

Behind his mustache, Colonel Abercrombie's lips twisted in wry amusement.

"It seems he has a lady friend in town, and he didn't want his mother to know he'd spent the evening with her."

I gaped. "He would rather have hanged than confess that he had a sweetheart?"

The colonel shrugged. "A mother's disapproval can be a heavy burden. Also, he knew he was innocent. I suppose he thought he'd be acquitted based on the case's merits, and if he wasn't, well, he'd cross that bridge when he got there."

"I suppose," I said. Colonel Abercrombie leaned forward, linking his hands on his desk.

"Pryce laid much of the credit for Hope's apprehension at Miss Sherwood's feet," he said. "Was her contribution really so significant?"

"It was, sir," I said. "There would have been no apprehension if it weren't for her."

"Interesting," Colonel Abercrombie said thoughtfully. "Most interesting indeed."

I breathed deeply, recognizing an opening for the topic that had dominated my thoughts since my last conversation with the lady in question.

"Colonel," I said. "Am I correct in thinking that Pryce included a full account of Lieutenant Drebber's actions in his report?"

He settled back in his chair, giving me an assessing look.

"He did."

"Drebber..." I began, then realized I wasn't sure what to say next. I licked my lips and tried again. "Hope, of course, deserves to be prosecuted to the full extent of the law, but Drebber's conduct was... not what one would hope for from an officer in Her Majesty's army."

Colonel Abercrombie raised an eyebrow. "I won't—I can't—dispute that assertion on its face. But what compels you to bring it up in this context?"

"Surely, there is something that could be done—some recognition of the wrongs that he perpetrated against multiple innocents, including a young Folk woman."

He sighed. "And what would you suggest, doctor? As distasteful as they were, his actions were not illegal."

"I understand, sir —"

"And even if they had been, the man is dead. There is no further penance for him to serve."

"So, his name remains clear? In the eyes of the nation, he still deserves the rights and honors that are part and partial to a commission in the army? Is it too much to ask that the wronged woman's family get some acknowledgement of the wrong perpetrated against her and a modicum of justice for it, especially in light of the political climate here on the island?"

The colonel's face softened, but rather than mollifying me, this demonstration of pity cut like a knife. "Dr. Jarvis, I understand your concerns—truly, I do. But what you suggest is beyond the scope of our duties. If the army became embroiled in every instance of an officer fathering a by-blow on a pretty girl who'd caught his eye, we wouldn't have time to defend the nation."

I clasped my hands in front of me, letting my eyes slide to the carpet at my feet.

"Get to work, doctor," he said, not unkindly. "I'm sure there will be more to discuss on this matter in the future, but there's nothing to be done about it now."

I nodded and left the room.

I spent the morning huddled in my office, pretending to work. I heard Waddington come in—the colonel was right, he did sound like a drunk horse—and I thought I heard Pryce's voice at some point, too, though I couldn't be sure. I kept my head down, stewing, until a light knock came at my door. Looking up, I saw Miss Sherwood standing there.

"May I come in?"

I grunted something that could have been interpreted as either negative or affirmative. She took it as the latter, stepping inside and taking a seat in a chair in front of my desk. I felt a flash of alarm, having her in such close quarters, again unchaperoned, but the door was open. Her presence would likely go unremarked, and even if it didn't, I wasn't in the mood to be concerned about it.

"Why are you here?" I asked, more abruptly than was strictly polite. I knew she couldn't have had any notion of my discussion with the colonel, but it still felt as if she'd come to gloat.

"I only wanted to see if you had heard that Mr. Hope had passed."

Her words caught me up short, and I laid the paper I was holding aside.

"I had not heard that."

She nodded. "The aneurysm burst, as he told us it would."

"Who told you?" I asked. "Did you visit the jail?" Then I paused, noting suddenly that she was still dressed in the same clothes as the day before. "Have you even been to sleep?"

She shook her head. "I have not. And Hope never made it to the jail. Pryce and the magistrate decided it was too dangerous to move him." I felt a pang of shame then, that I had let my emotions get in the way of being there to play my role in making that call, and her next words did nothing to assuage it. "He died in that room at the boarding house."

"How do you know this?"

"I was there. I stayed to sit with Mr. Hope."

My eyebrows shot up in surprise. "What? Why?"

Miss Sherwood gave something that was not quite a shrug. "I was very interested in his friend's formulation of opium. He obligingly answered my questions, at least until talking became too difficult. But I also thought to provide him with some company." She paused. "I hoped it might bring some comfort to his final hours. Not being alone."

"He was a murderer," I said. "Many would assert that he did not deserve comfort."

She gazed at me levelly. "Many are cruel and immoderately smug regarding their own character and conduct."

I sat back in my chair, considering her.

"Do you think his actions justified?"

"No," she said. "But I understand his motivations."

And I did too, now. Because Hope's justice *was* all the justice Marina was ever going to get. Miss Sherwood had been right, and I knew it, and it still made me angry. But it was not her fault that she was right. As she'd told me before—had it only been two days?—she only reported what she saw. She couldn't help that what she saw was ugly.

Perhaps she understood something of my musings, because she got to her feet.

"I should be going. As I said, I only wanted to tell you about Mr. Hope."

"Thank you," I said, standing as well. "I appreciate the gesture."

She nodded, and I caught a glint of light at her throat.

"Your necklace," I said, almost without thinking. "Why did you choose it? I noticed you wore a snake pendant at the ball as well."

Her hand strayed absently to the chain.

"There's a Bible verse my grandmother likes to quote. Matthew 10:16. 'Behold, I send you forth as sheep in the midst of wolves. Be ye therefore wise as serpents and harmless as doves.' I try to use it as a guide to my conduct."

I gazed at her. "A worthy goal. It suits you."

She laughed softly. "I do my best."

I nodded. "I hope we will meet again soon, Miss Sherwood."

She gave me a smile with a glint of mischief in it.

"Oh, I suspect we shall. It is, after all, not a very large island," and then she left.

Looking back on the last few days, I can see this ordeal has changed me in ways I could not have predicted. For the first time in a long time, I have felt capable. Useful. And while I fully expect life here to revert to the mundane routine I described, I find the prospect does not weigh on me so heavily. I understand the significance of what happens on this tiny island in a way I didn't before, and I plan to do what I can to make this alliance succeed.

And if I do happen to run into Miss Sherwood again…
so much the better.

Your brother,
Wilf

Wilf, Honoria, and the other residents of Ynis Within will return in the summer of 2024.

In the meantime, you can sign up for my newsletter to get information about new releases, cool extras, and other fun stuff at www.reneeed wardsauthor.com.

Also by Renee Edwards

A POWERFUL PROHIBITION

To the Stars

Author's Note

For such a little book, *A Puzzle of Poppies* felt like it required an outsized amount of research. Granted, that research will carry over to future stories about Wilf and Honoria, so it wasn't all just in service of this humble novella, but still – I had to get everything in place to establish the world moving forward, and it was A Lot. I was viscerally reminded why I decided to set my novel series, A Powerful Prohibition, in a secondary world where I have the ability to just make random stuff up!

I realize now that I went in a bit cocky, thinking I'd absorbed most of what I needed to write this book by consuming copious amount of stories (in both print and film) set in the period. To a certain extent this was true, but I quickly realized I didn't know quite as much as I thought I did. So the research commenced! While the sheer amount of it was daunting, the process itself is my happy place; I was, after all, a librarian in my previous life. I picked up bibs and bobs from all over, but there were a few resources that I relied upon especially heavily and returned to again and again, and I would like to share those with you here.

General Information Related to the Period and Setting

Books:

- *Daily Life in Victorian England, 2ⁿᵈ ed.* by Sally Mitchell
- *The Writer's Guide to Everyday Life in Regency and Victorian England from 1811-1901* by Kristin Hughes
- *Daughters of Britannia: The Lives and Times of Diplomatic Wives* by Katie Hickman

Digital Archives:

- JSTOR – Academic papers galore!
- Project Gutenberg and The Wellcome Collection – Treasure troves of 19th century primary resources. The latter was especially invaluable for topics related to science and medicine.

Wilf's Travels and Military Service

- The Second Anglo-Afghan War 1878-1880 – This very detailed and comprehensive website was indispensable when considering Wilf's experiences in India and Afghanistan. It even has an article discussing how accurate Arthur Conan Doyle was in his portrayal of Dr. Watson's military service in *A Study in Scarlet* (spoiler alert: not very).
- British Battles: The Battle of Maiwand – Another good resource on Afghanistan
- "MAIWAND, 27th July 1880" by Brian Robson - Accessed via JSTOR
- "The travel writers of colonial India left us with remarkable images" by Mridula Chari – This article directed me to some excellent examples

of Victorian British travel writing about the East that I was then able to track down via the Internet Archive.

The Folk

- *Strange and Secret Peoples: Fairies and Victorian Consciousness* by Carole G. Silver – This was by far the resource I leaned on the most for lore and insight into the relationship between traditional folk belief and Victorian attitudes and values.
- British Fairies
- Myth and Moor – This is author and folklorist Terri Wilding's site, and it contains tons of great information.
- The geography of Ynis Witrin is based on that of real tidal islands from around the world, most notably Mont-Saint-Michel in France and St. Michael's Mount in Cornwall (and, if I'm being entirely honest, a tiny bit on the island of Pabu from *The Bad Batch*).

Even with all of this information at my fingertips, I've sure I've made some errors, and that knowledge haunts me. I am especially plagued by the worry that in sweating tiny details, I have missed something big and obvious (and humiliating). But you have to let things go at some point. I hope you have enjoyed your foray into Wilf and Honoria's world so far and that you will visit again in the future!

Renee Edwards
2024

About the Author

Renee is a lifelong book person and trained librarian. Her favorite books to read are the kind with magic, adventure, and romance, so those are what she set out to write. She fiddles away on her laptop in Texas, where she lives with her husband and a basset hound named Winifred.